TOM SWIFT AND HIS GIANT ROBOT

THE NEW TOM SWIFT JR. ADVENTURES

BY VICTOR APPLETON II

TOM SWIFT AND HIS FLYING LAB
TOM SWIFT AND HIS JETMARINE
TOM SWIFT AND HIS ROCKET SHIP
TOM SWIFT AND HIS GIANT ROBOT
TOM SWIFT AND HIS ATOMIC EARTH BLASTER
TOM SWIFT AND HIS OUTPOST IN SPACE
TOM SWIFT AND HIS DIVING SEACOPTER
TOM SWIFT IN THE CAVES OF NUCLEAR FIRE
TOM SWIFT ON THE PHANTOM SATELLITE

Sermek side-stepped but not far enough

THE NEW TOM SWIFT JR. ADVENTURES

TOM SWIFT

AND HIS GIANT ROBOT

BY VICTOR APPLETON II

ILLUSTRATED BY GRAHAM KAYE

GROSSET & DUNLAP

NEW YORK PUBLISHERS

PRINTED IN THE UNITED STATES OF AMERICA

CONTENTS

CONTENTS

ILLUSTRATIONS

TOM SWIFT AND HIS GIANT ROBOT

CHAPTER 1

THE PHANTOM JET

"HEY, Tom, take it easy! We can stand only so many G's, you know."

"Okay, Bud."

Tom Swift pulled back on the wheel of his diving jet plane. He had just dropped from thin air into the troposphere. Now, leveling off his delta-wing craft, the eighteen-year-old inventor grinned at the protesting voice from his friend seated directly behind him.

"What's the matter, pal? Seventy thousand feet too much for you?"

"It's the way you come down, Tom. My stomach feels as if I'd left it in space."

"It's all for science," Tom said, chuckling, as he guided the craft in a sweeping arc toward the town of Shopton.

Bud smiled. "Next time you're going so high to test out a gimmick for that giant robot of yours,

1

Tom, why don't you take the old rivet-head himself along?"

"Smile when you call my robot names," Tom growled with mock ferocity.

Both boys looked like well-padded fullbacks with oversized helmets. Inside their flight gear, however, they were quite different. Tom, lean, tall, and with a blond crew cut, had a serious look in his deep-set blue eyes as he scanned the horizon. Bud, a skilled pilot himself, was not as tall as Tom, but he had shoulders like a hammer thrower and the open, frank face of an athlete who liked to play for fun.

"The worst is over," Tom called through his mike. "But keep buckled in tight. I'm making another dive before I take her in. But I warn you, next time we're going higher, where we'll get hit harder by cosmic rays. It'll be a better test of the effect of radiation on the relotrol."

Tom glanced at a black metal box with three dials resting in his lap. It contained the receiver of a control instrument to be used in connection with the giant robot he was building. Tom had partially completed the mechanical giant to be used for repairs and maintenance in a new atomic energy plant which his father was building. The relotrol would relay radio impulses needed to guide the robot working in areas of the plant where the radiation would be fatal to human beings.

"How did your gimmick react, Tom?" Bud asked.

"Not good. I'll have to make some changes. Under

really stiff radiation this relotrol would foul up the radio orders to the robot."

Bud grinned. "You mean Mr. Robot wouldn't know what to do? He'd sort of go berserk?"

"Right."

"Well, what's next on the program, inventor boy?"

"To work on the relotrol some more," Tom replied. He clamped his invention under the instrument panel to keep it from being jarred, then nosed the plane down in the direction of the Swift Enterprises airfield.

Below was the town of Shopton, with the old Swift Construction Company buildings on one side and the new experimental group on the other. The shiny rooftops of the laboratories reflected the morning sun.

"Swift Enterprises looks mighty enterprising!" Bud said. "Do you feel enterprising enough to work the bugs out of the relotrol right now?"

"As soon as we land, Bud," Tom said, looking down.

But Bud's eyes were not on the airfield. They were following a black dot that had suddenly appeared against the horizon.

"Something's coming at us from three o'clock," he said. "It's too small to be a plane."

The speck quickly increased in size.

"It's a bird," said Bud in amazement. "A large black crow."

Tom climbed a few hundred feet to avoid hitting

it, then cut the jet's speed. As the bird winged below him, he said, "That's too big for a crow. It's larger than an eagle."

"But it *is* a crow," cried Bud.

Tom looked again and caught his breath. The bird was immense. It was shaped exactly like a crow but was larger than a vulture. The monstrous bird glided through the sky, then wheeled.

"I'd like to get a close look at him," Bud said.

"I'm not sure that would be safe," Tom replied warily. "The bird might panic and fly into one of our control surfaces."

He banked away from it. The bird, however, flew even closer to the plane.

"I'm going to get a picture of it," Bud said, slipping one arm free of his parachute harness and reaching for a camera he had put in a forward compartment. "May be a prize shot. Put her into a slow circle and hold her steady, Tom."

"Steady as she goes," Tom replied, grinning.

His expert knowledge of aircraft was one of the many technical skills possessed by the young scientist. Bud knew that Tom could keep the plane as stable in flight as it was when standing on a runway.

Loosening his chute still further, Bud peered through the range finder and focused the lens on the crow. He was about to trip the shutter when the plane suddenly lurched violently. Bud banged his head against the canopy.

"What happened?" he yelled.

A look of worry creased Tom's forehead. "She went out of control, Bud. Must have hit an air pocket."

As he checked the automatic horizon, the ship flipped into a series of erratic rolls and sideslips.

"Hey! What's—?" Bud's cries were choked off as he gasped for breath.

Tom worked frantically. "The controls aren't responding right, Bud. I'm going to try for altitude."

He pulled back on the wheel but the plane did not rise. Instead, it pivoted slowly and began to move in the opposite direction, away from Shopton.

"It seems to be on a planned course!" Tom cried, half stunned by the ship's ghostlike actions.

Tom struggled desperately to regain control of the plane. He reduced the fuel flow but the ship continued to pick up speed. When he tried to dive, the craft pointed straight ahead!

"For the love of Mike," Bud exclaimed, "what's going on?"

"I'm trying to figure it out," Tom replied tersely. "Sit tight!"

Tom used every bit of flying knowledge he possessed, but the plane ignored every attempt to bring it under control.

"Can't you bring her down?" Bud asked frantically.

"No. Something has kayoed our control instruments," Tom answered. "But we still have one chance. I may be able to stall her and glide in."

Tom reached down and pulled a gear handle. The plane's wing flaps slowly spread open and the jet slowed for a moment. Then, as if angered by this latest move, the craft went into a tail spin. Over and over it spiraled toward the ground.

"Bud!" Tom yelled. "Jump!"

Desperately Bud tried to tighten his parachute harness which had loosened when he reached for his camera.

Meanwhile, Tom was fighting to release the hatch. It, too, seemed to be under the influence of the strange force. Below him, the earth was spinning crazily and every instant the patches of green-and-brown landscape leaped closer.

Tom knew he must act fast. Cutting the control wire leading to the hatch, he shorted it against another circuit. A crackle of sparks jumped across the cabin and the hatch in the floor sprang open. Automatically the seat ejectors were set off. First Bud, then Tom, was hurtled down and backward from the ship.

Tom counted and pulled the rip cord of his chute. Gripping the shroud lines, he started turning around in mid-air to search for his friend.

The sky below him was empty. But several hundred feet away he saw Bud, almost parallel to himself. Bud waved to signal that he was all right.

"Thank goodness!" Tom breathed. Then, gazing about for the plane, he muttered, "I hate to see that jet crack up. And it's the end of the relotrol."

His thoughts were suddenly distracted by a roaring swish. Looking below, Tom gasped at the miracle taking place.

The tail-spinning plane had righted itself! Now the empty aircraft was flying in a straight course away from Shopton!

CHAPTER 2

THE HEADLESS GIANT

THEIR PARACHUTES buffeted by the wind, Tom and Bud stared in bewilderment as the pilotless jet flew into the distance. The great black crow was homing in alongside the deserted craft.

"If I could only follow it!" Tom thought in disgust. "But I'll get some pictures of it."

Quickly he reached into the large supply pouch on his parachute harness which contained a combination camera and a small two-way radio tuned to the frequency of the control tower at Swift Enterprises.

He set the lens and managed to snap two shots of the plane and the bird before they flew out of range. Now he flipped the switch on the radio and in a moment an answer came.

"Get this message to Slim Davis pronto," Tom said to the tower operator. Slim excelled in handling

8

high-speed aircraft and had proved invaluable in several emergencies.

Tom quickly briefed the tower attendant on the mysterious episode, saying, "I want Slim to find that plane. It took a westerly direction. There's an invention of mine on board that I'd hate to lose."

"A spook plane!" the operator exclaimed. "I'll phone Slim at once. Roger."

A few seconds later Tom hit the ground, somersaulted easily, and collapsed his parachute. Bud came up carrying his folded chute while Tom was radioing directions to the tower for picking them up.

"Of all the weird things!" Bud exclaimed. "First I thought the jet's controls had been wrecked. But then it pulls out of the spin and flies off!"

"Something was out to get the plane and not us," Tom replied. "Otherwise, why force us to bail out first?"

"You're right there. Say, how much of that little episode did you get on film?"

"Only a couple of shots. I wonder if they'll prove anything."

"What gets me," said Bud, "is that crow. Do you think it had anything to do with kidnaping the jet?"

Tom looked thoughtfully into space. "Right now, I don't see how it could have."

A short time later a jeep arrived to take the boys to Shopton. They asked Morton, the driver, if any word from Slim Davis had come over the jeep's short-wave radio.

"Not a thing," Morton answered, and no report came during the drive.

When they reached the Enterprises grounds, Tom and Bud went directly to the large private office the young inventor and his father shared. They were amazed to find Mr. Swift there.

"Dad!" Tom exclaimed, rushing up to him. "Good to have you back."

Mr. Swift had just returned from his atomic energy plant under construction in the western United States. The elder scientist, whose own discoveries and inventions had led him on many fascinating adventures, was not quite as tall as his six-foot son. But in many other ways, the resemblance between father and son was obvious.

He shook hands with the boys and said, "What's this I hear about your plane taking off by itself?"

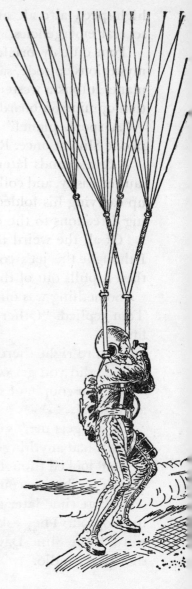

Tom outlined the mysterious episode for his father while Bud developed the pictures in an adjoining darkroom. When Bud returned with the slides, Tom said, "I'll put them in the projector." He crossed to his own desk, pressed a button, and watched a screen slide down into place against the far wall. At the same time, shutters dropped over the windows and the lights dimmed. Tom inserted the two slides and turned on the viewing light.

He managed to snap two shots of the plane and the bird

"This first picture—" said Tom hopefully, then stopped. The distant aerial shot which appeared on the screen was too faint to make out details and the focus was blurred. "Mm-m, that's not much help," he murmured, turning the viewer.

"The next one is a close-up of the crow," Bud said.

The sharp image of the giant black bird filled the picture area. Everyone gasped and Tom cried:

"That's no bird!"

"It certainly isn't," said Mr. Swift incredulously. "Those aren't feathers at all. They look like jet tubes. That's some sort of missile designed to look like a crow."

The three studied the picture. Then Tom switched off the projector and adjusted the lights.

"Maybe it's a guiding robot," said Tom thoughtfully. He snapped his fingers. "Do you suppose that it could be from our space friends?"

Tom referred to mysterious beings in outer space who some time ago had sent a meteorlike object plunging to the grounds of Swift Enterprises. On it were geometric figures which Tom and his father had translated, and later Mr. Swift had compiled a space dictionary from them. Messages had been sent and answers received on oscillograph screens, both at the plant and on board Tom's rocket ship.

"They might have sent the missile disguised as a type of earth bird so as not to frighten people," Bud suggested.

Mr. Swift shook his head. "I believe that they

would have contacted us first. But it wouldn't hurt to send a message to them at once."

"I hope they're in a position to pick up our beam," said Tom as he flipped on the scope and sent a small, then a large circle, followed by a series of interlocking triangles—the identification code used by the space beings. Tom now sent symbols asking if the strange bird belonged to them.

Bud and the Swifts waited eagerly. For a few minutes the oscillograph remained blank, then green mathematical symbols began to appear in rapid succession.

Before the Swifts had a chance to decipher them, Miss Trent, their secretary, buzzed the phone to say that Mr. Swift was wanted on long-distance. He switched the instrument to the out-of-town call.

Bud leaned toward Tom and whispered, "What do they say?"

"Just a second, chum." Tom was skimming rapidly through the space dictionary. He knew many of the symbol combinations by heart and could translate whole paragraphs without referring to the book. But some of these symbols were new to him and he wanted to make sure that he had correctly translated the message. The sending ceased. Tom jotted down a few notes.

"That's odd," he said, a note of apprehension in his voice.

"Well, give boy!" cried Bud. "What did they say?"

"It wasn't their crow, Bud. Our space friends don't know anything about it."

"Did it take all this time to tell you that?"

Tom grinned. "No, Bud. They said that they're still waiting for directions from us to enable them to penetrate the earth's atmosphere and stay alive."

Mr. Swift had put down the phone and now he commented, "We'll never be able to help these spacemen to visit us until they describe their body structure to us."

"I've asked them that many times," said Tom. "Maybe they haven't figured out what we want to know. But right now I have a problem that's more important. Their answer must mean the jet crow was from earth."

"It may have carried some kind of beamer that activated your automatic pilot," said Mr. Swift.

Bud, perplexed, ran his fingers through his hair. "What does it all mean?"

Tom looked grim. "I'd say somebody is out to steal the secrets of my giant robot. And he may have the relotrol already!"

The desk buzzer sounded again and Miss Trent reported that Slim Davis had found no trace of the missing jet from the air and was returning to Shopton. Tom was disappointed. The mystery was deepening.

"I'm going on a search myself," he declared. "Come on, Bud!"

"Take it easy," his father warned.

"We will, Dad."

The two young fliers hurried off and in a short time were air-borne. Bud radioed all airports in a five-hundred-mile radius to learn if the jet had been landed, but in each case the answer was No.

Meanwhile, Tom glided his small jet plane through the skies, passing several ships in his circular route. There was no sign of the missing craft. Discouraged, he headed back to Shopton.

"No telling what happened," Bud remarked. "Maybe the jet blew up!"

Tom nodded, brought the plane to a smooth landing, and taxied to the hangar.

"If so, my relotrol's gone for good," he said, as the two boys got out.

"And I'd sure like to know where that crow came from," Bud added, then said, "See you later, pal. I'll be over at the radio tower checking out the new transmitter."

Tom hurried back to his office, where Mr. Swift was speaking into a dictating machine. His son gathered that it was part of a report on certain phases of the new atomic energy plant.

As the young inventor waited for his father to finish, he gazed around the spacious, well-lighted room. Back of Mr. Swift's desk hung pictures of faraway places the elder inventor had visited in his younger days. Beside him, in a vast glass cabinet, were bronze models of a dirigible, a great searchlight, a war tank, and a model of a small motorcycle.

On a stand near Tom's desk was a large, accurately scaled model of his jetmarine, the *Sea Dart,* which had carried him and Bud on a Caribbean adventure after modern pirates. The atomic-powered submarine had been hand-tooled in blue plastic by Arvid Hanson, head of the Swifts' modelmaking division.

At its side was another example of Hanson's craftmanship—a bright yellow model of Tom's rocket ship, the *Star Spear,* resting on three red fins. In it Tom and Bud had entered a space race. A third model rested on his massive desk. This one was his favorite—a large silver reproduction of his Flying Lab.

"Well, Tom, how did you make out?" Mr. Swift asked, clicking off the dictating machine.

"The plane has completely vanished, Dad. If it did land, it's well hidden."

Mr. Swift walked to his son's side and laid a hand on his shoulder. "Don't let this mystery take all of your time. I'll need that giant robot pretty soon. How is work on it progressing?"

"He's still headless." Tom grinned. "But from his neck down he works well. Want to see him?"

"Indeed I do."

Mr. Swift followed his son along a corridor, then both stepped onto a conveyor belt. Picking up speed, the moving floor rapidly transported them to the main wing of the laboratory building. They entered Tom's metallurgy and electronics laboratory, filled with motors, workbenches, and lathes. In a corner stood the giant lifelike robot.

Even without its "head," the gleaming, silver-gray automaton stood seven feet tall. Tomasite, the young inventor's wonder plastic, covered every part of its frame except the joints. These were enclosed in "sleeves" of fine Tomasite chain mail which stretched and contracted with the movements of the joints.

"I suppose the transmitting and receiving antenna will be in the head?" Mr. Swift asked.

"Right, along with the television 'eyes' and radio 'ears.' After the giant's head is on, he'll be remotely controlled. Right now," Tom went on, pointing to a cable protruding from the back of the robot's neck and running to a control panel on the wall, "I have to use a direct control and monitoring method."

"What can your giant do so far?" Mr. Swift asked.

"Walk, and do almost anything with his hands. Want to see him thread a needle?"

Mr. Swift smiled. "I'd rather watch him walk."

"Okay. Here goes." Tom set the panel for "walking" and slipped in a punched tape to control arm-and-hand motions. He explained that the perforated tapes, which would be used for the robot's various actions and motions, operated on the same principle as a player-piano roll.

The young inventor turned a key to open the relay circuits in the robot and the giant's machinery began to hum. At the same time, its body broke out into a blaze of dazzling colored lights.

Mr. Swift roared with laughter. "A real show with lights. What are they for?"

"I installed bulbs of various colors at the joints to tell me how the circuits are working," Tom explained as he snapped off the laboratory lights.

Mr. Swift chuckled. "Looks like a Christmas tree."

"But who ever saw a *walking* Christmas tree?" Tom grinned. "Watch this!"

He advanced the "walking" dial on the control board a few notches. Slowly the robot lifted his right foot. The foot moved forward, paused, and came down with a crunch. Memory tapes in the control panel sent a signal to the other foot, moving it just far enough to avoid toppling the body. Step by step, the automaton moved forward.

Tom stepped up the speed and the giant began to move very fast.

"Look out!" Mr. Swift warned. "It's going pretty rapidly."

Tom chuckled. "If he gets going faster than the volume control calls for, a damper will automatically slow him down."

The robot was almost running now.

"Tom, he's going to walk into that vacuum furnace!" his father warned.

Laughing, Tom quickly threw a switch for a coordinated turn. The giant stopped. Sensory readers on the control panel checked patterns of holes in the tapes for instructions. Then he pivoted.

Mr. Swift looked relieved. The robot now headed for the closed door leading to the corridor. Again he was going at breakneck speed. Mr. Swift held his breath but Tom seemed confident.

Working quickly, he inserted a special-action tape in a slot in the control panel. The metal body paused, raised its right arm, and extended the hand. Two metal fingers reached out, found the doorknob, and turned it slowly.

Stepping forward, the giant pushed it open. The arm mechanism dropped and the robot paused.

"Watch him take this without stumbling," Tom said, running to the door and laying a section of five-inch pipe across the opening.

Bending slightly, his lights flashing, the giant stepped neatly over the pipe and strode into the silent corridor.

Suddenly Tom and his father froze as an unearthly shriek sounded in the hall and echoed through the laboratory.

CHAPTER 3

AMAZING FINGERPRINTS

"QUICK, Tom! Stop him!" Mr. Swift cried.

Tom frantically slammed down a switch on the control board to halt the robot. As the giant stabilized, Tom and his father rushed in front of him. A stupefied man stood there, his mouth wide open.

"Brand my lil ole panhandle!" he exclaimed. "I thought some Texas Ranger's ghost was goin' to tackle me!"

"Chow!" roared Tom, a broad smile of relief spreading over his face. "You old coyote cooker! When did you ride into town?"

"Jest tumbled in an' I don't recollect you ever eatin' any o' my coyote cutlets, Tom Swift!"

Chow Winkler, the stout, former chuck-wagon cook who tended the galley on the Flying Lab and went along on many of Tom's journeys, mopped his forehead with a large red neckerchief. "Whew!" he said. "Feller can't even come lopin' along your conveyor belt without gettin' skeered half to death."

"So you haven't met Tom's giant?" Mr. Swift said. "Where have you been, Chow?"

"Visitin' some ranch friends. Woulda stayed, too, if I'd knowed I was goin' to bump into this here monster. What is it anyway, Tom?"

"A robot that will move and act like a person," Tom explained. "Only difference is that my mechanical man will work where it's too dangerous for a human being to go."

Warily Chow moved closer to the robot. "That sounds real good, Tom," he drawled. Eying its immensity, he said, "Glad I don't have to cook for this here giant. Say, maybe you-all could rig up one o' these come roundup time next year in Texas. My friends sure could use a mee-chanical cowpuncher for ropin' an' brandin'."

"I'll do better than that, Chow," said Tom, laughing. "How about my entering one in the Southwest Rodeo for you? I'll fix the controls so he'll never get thrown by any bronc!"

"That's right nice o' you, Tom," said Chow, grinning. "Tell you what. He kin wear my new red-an'-yellow plaid shirt. He'd sure look more civilized that way."

"But we'll wait until he has a head," said Tom. "I'd hate to scare your cowboy friends."

"Say, I'll bet a lil ole prairie dog you folks ain't had lunch. How 'bout a bowl o' my rattlesnake soup?" he asked jokingly.

"No, thanks," said Tom. "I'd rather be bitten by a new idea. *That* I could use!"

"Reckon I could cook up most everythin' but that!" Chow waved to the scientists and entered the private laboratory galley of which he was the proud master.

While Chow prepared a substantial lunch of hamburgers and onions, the Swifts tried further experiments with the robot. Then, after eating, the two inventors separated. Mr. Swift returned to his office, while Tom worked in his laboratory on plans for improving the relotrol.

At six o'clock he returned to his office and learned that his father had gone home. At this moment Bud dashed in.

"I have news!" he reported excitedly. "Slim finally located the plane, after all. He combed the area in a jeep and found the jet hidden in a woods about ten miles from here."

"What!" Tom cried. "That close? Was anyone seen near it?"

"Slim says that the plane seems deserted, but he's waiting for you before going aboard."

Tom grabbed his two-way short-wave set. In a moment he was talking to Slim, getting exact directions to the spot in the woods where the jet had been located.

"I'll be right over with a crew," Tom told him. "Stay around but don't get too close. This may be a trap."

Tom clicked off the set and called Phil Radnor, chief security police officer of the Enterprises plant. Radnor said that he would organize a group of reliable men and join the boys at the main entrance gate.

A motorcade was formed and was soon weaving a rapid but careful path through the highway traffic outside Shopton. Up front in a jeep were Tom and Bud. Seated behind them, alert and ready for any sudden action, sat Radnor and a guard. The second vehicle contained several mechanics and laborers.

Following it was a large truck pulling an aircraft trailer. To the top of this flat conveyance an entire plane, with the wings dismantled, could be lashed and towed away.

The cavalcade swung off the main highway onto a narrow, rutted road, densely lined with trees whose branches intertwined overhead. The pace of the vehicles slowed down and their headlights stabbed through the gathering dusk, groping around bends in the road.

Slim was waiting in the shadows. He guided the boys and the security guards on foot through the woods and into a long, narrow clearing. At the end of it stood Tom's jet plane, the forward half between giant trees with spreading branches. Tom swung himself onto the right wing. Cautiously he made his

way to the canopy and beamed his flashlight inside.
No one was aboard.

"The bubble's open. I'm going inside," Tom said.

He lifted the canopy and stepped down into the
plane. Bud followed. A quick look around revealed
that nothing had been damaged, but the relotrol
was missing.

"Stolen!" Tom declared.

"Could it have fallen out?" suggested Bud hopefully.

"Not a chance. I'll bet that it was taken by the
same person who was manipulating the crow."

Bud looked incredulous. "But who would want
your relotrol, Tom?"

"I don't know, Bud, but I mean to find out! Rad
probably brought a fingerprint kit. We'll use that."

Cautiously he made his way to the canopy

Tom called to the security officer and asked him. "Yes, I have one," Radnor replied. "I'll get it."

When he returned the security officer dusted the cockpit interior and certain surface sections of the fuselage. A number of fingerprints appeared.

"No doubt some of these belong to you boys," he said. "But there seem to be several different sets of prints. We'll take them all."

After the prints had been lifted, Radnor said, "We'll compare these with the file at the plant. Any unknown ones we'll check with the local police. If they can't help, we'll fly them to Washington at once for identification."

Phil Radnor started back to the plant immediately. Tom and Bud remained to supervise the work of removing the plane. First the men had to cut

and beamed his flashlight inside

through the woods, hacking out a path for the trailer truck with electric saws. This accomplished, they drove the truck in and the task of dismantling the triangular-shaped wings began. Finally everything was loaded and the plane was returned to its berth at Swift Enterprises.

Tom and Bud immediately began an inspection of the motors, cables, and electrical equipment. There was not a clue to the strange kidnaping.

"There's only one chance of finding out who did this," Tom said.

"What's that?"

"The fingerprints."

"It'll turn out that they belong to some scientific crook like those international spies you captured," Bud ventured.

The young inventor shrugged. Then, before he could make a reply, Bud exclaimed, "Do you know what time it is? Nine o'clock and we haven't had any dinner! Go on home, genius, and feed that brain of yours."

"Okay."

Tom dropped Bud off at an aunt's with whom he had been staying, since Bud's parents now lived in California. Then Tom drove to his own large, comfortable home. As he pulled into the garage he met his sister Sandra just coming from the kennels where the Swifts kept two fine bloodhounds.

"Hi, Sis! What's for dinner?" Tom asked.

"You mean what *was* for dinner, Tom. We had

steak and French fried potatoes," said Sandy. She was a year younger than Tom and had the same light-colored hair and blue eyes as her brother. She laughed. "I'll fix something for you."

"Thanks, Sis. You'll save my life! Boy, I'm starved!"

They walked into the house together and Tom went at once to greet his pretty mother. She was in the living room with Mr. Swift.

"Sorry I'm so late," Tom said.

Mrs. Swift smiled. "I understand, dear. Your father thought you might be off hunting for the lost plane again."

"Yes, I was," he replied.

"How did you make out?" Mr. Swift asked, looking up from some papers he was reading.

They listened in amazement to their son's story. He concluded by saying, "The plane itself wasn't damaged, but my relotrol is gone. We dusted for fingerprints and—"

"Oh, say," Sandy interrupted, coming in from the kitchen. "Phil Radnor called you on the videophone just a few minutes ago. He wants to talk to you about fingerprint verification. He said that it was urgent, so I told him you'd call back as soon as you came in."

Tom reached for the direct private videophone coaxial to the plant. He waited while one of his operators in the main building terminal made the switching connections on the huge cable board, which linked the company's coast-to-coast private television network. When Radnor's face appeared on the screen, he looked excited and distraught.

"What is it, Rad?" Tom asked.

"I have a report for you from the police. Some of the prints identified belong to an escaped Federal prisoner!"

"What!"

"He's 'Flash' Ludens of the Briggin gang."

"The Briggin gang!" Tom exclaimed. "They're the cleverest, most dangerous bank robbers at large today!"

"That's the outfit," Radnor said. "The other two members are 'Slick' Steck and 'Pins' Zoltan."

Tom was completely mystified. "Rad," he said slowly, "what would bank robbers want with my relotrol? It doesn't make sense!"

CHAPTER 4

MENACING BIRDS

BY MORNING not only the Swift family but the whole Enterprises organization was buzzing with the exciting news that a well-known bank robber, and perhaps his confederates, was now an enemy of Tom's.

In his office, the young inventor was talking with Bud, Radnor, and young Harlan Ames, head of the plant's security division. They were looking at rogues' gallery pictures of the Briggin gang supplied by the Shopton police.

"They're not a very pretty crew," commented Ames. "But they make up for it with their clever trickery." The security chief smiled wryly. "According to reports, this Briggin mob has made a peculiar switch of operations—graduated from guns to science, it seems. They now call themselves gentlemen scientists of the underworld."

Radnor pointed to one of the photos. "This tall, dark one, Flash Ludens, the trio's ringleader, is an electrical wizard."

Tom studied the face as Bud burst out, "Say, look at Flash's hair. Some plastering job!"

"Good reason for it," Ames said. "Covers a jagged scar running almost the length of his scalp."

"What about these other two characters?" Tom asked.

"Pins Zoltan, the short, blond one, used to be a crackerjack bank robber," Ames went on. "One day, though, while he was backing out of a bank with gun drawn, an armored truck pulled up on an unscheduled stop. The guards blazed away and Zoltan's spine was nicked by a bullet. Today two metal surgical pins still remain in his backbone. That's how he got his nickname."

"And this dark-haired one with the mustache," Radnor took up the story, "he's Slick Steck—a real gangland product."

Ames nodded. "They don't come any tougher than Slick."

Abruptly Tom swung out of his chair. There was a grim look on his face. "I'm starting to get the shape of things now. The Briggin boys' change to science is a lot more sinister than their bank robberies."

Ames looked grave. "I'm afraid you're right, Tom."

"With Flash Ludens—the brain—calling the formula, he and the other two are probably making a mint of money selling scientific information and apparatus to other mobsters."

"So that's their racket," Bud commented. "But I still don't see what they want with Tom's relotrol."

No one could answer this, but Tom said tersely, "That's something we'd better hurry and find out."

"Okay, pal," Bud replied. "How do we start?"

"By finding that mechanized crow," Tom answered. "If we discover it is remote controlled, we can trace the control beam and locate the operator's headquarters. Let's go, Bud." He strode toward the office door. "If anything else comes up," he said to Harlan and Radnor, "we'll be at the *Sky Queen's* hangar."

"Right," Ames said. "In the meantime, I'll alert the plant's security network."

As the boys hurried off toward the Flying Lab's mammoth underground hangar, Bud said, "So we're going to use the *Sky Queen* for this crow hunt."

"Yes. I figure on making a reconnaissance flight in the area where we were attacked."

"Whoever's directing the crow may not send it out against the Flying Lab, though," said Bud.

"I think we can make them."

"How?"

"By putting one of our robot models on board— a working model. They'd never pass up a chance to try capturing one of them."

"A robot lure, eh?" Bud laughed, then sobered. "But say, aren't you taking a chance that the Flying Lab will be kidnaped like the jet plane?"

"The Tomasite layers will protect us from any remote control, I'm sure."

Tom gave orders for the *Sky Queen* to be taken out, asking that as much publicity as possible be given to this to notify his enemy. Within a few minutes there was a bustle of activity. Men in gray coveralls scrambled around the roof of the huge hangar. Soon, to the whine of hydraulic lifts, the roof of the building split in two, each part rolling into the walls, and its subsurface floor rose toward the concrete apron.

A huge, gleaming stabilizer fin lifted into view. Then the immense body and wings appeared. The ship rested parallel to the ground on its tricycle landing gear.

"They're putting on a good show," Bud remarked.

Tom scanned the sky for any plane that might be hovering nearby, but there was none in sight. He hoped his plan would not be a failure.

"Let's go for the little robot now," he suggested to Bud.

As the boys started off, they met Chow and asked him if he wanted to go along and see the small robots in the model division. Tom explained that each robot had a special experimental function in connection with his giant robot.

"I reckon I kin stand it." The cook grinned.
"Mebbe one o' these lil ole robots will be better for
that rodeo than a giant."

The three entered a wing of one of the buildings
given over to modelmaking. They found six-foot,
heavy-set Arvid Hanson, head of this section, in his
office. He swiveled around on his workbench stool.
"Hello," he said. "Close the door behind you, Chow.
It's noisier than a boiler factory around here today."

Quickly Tom explained his plans and said he
wanted to put a walking robot aboard the *Sky Queen*
as a decoy.

"I hope the scheme will work," Hanson said. "But
watch out, Tom. This Briggin gang will stop at
nothing!"

Hanson led the way to a room where the midget
robots were kept.

Chow gasped. "Well, brand my circus side show!"
he exclaimed. "These ole dwarfs look mighty real
'cept for their funny box haids!"

"Wait until you see them work," Bud said. "How
about an exhibition, Arv?"

Hanson went to a control panel and dialed one
knob after another. At once the little mechanical
men began to perform. One walked, one raised and
lowered its arms, still another turned its head from
side to side and completely around.

Chow stared, dumfounded. "You didn't even
wind 'em up," he cried in disbelief.

"No, they're radio controlled," Tom answered.

"By the way, Arv, I want to take along a portable control panel on the Flying Lab to work Walter, the walking robot."

Hanson promised to have everything ready by four o'clock that afternoon and Tom said he would pick up Walter and the control panel himself.

Tom's next stop was at the Enterprises radio station, where he had a long talk with George Dilling, the manager.

They decided to use a system of triangulation. It was arranged that Dilling and his assistant would drive two radio-tracking trucks one hundred miles in different directions from Shopton. Both vehicles would be equipped with high-frequency signal detectors to trace the direction of the source of any instructions an enemy might send the crow. Another operator would remain at the Enterprises tower for the third detection point.

"Smith and I will leave at once," Dilling said, "so we'll be in position by the time you're aloft."

Tom, feeling that the final checkup on the arrangements for the reconnaissance flight could wait until afternoon, decided to go home to lunch. He invited Bud and together the boys left the Enterprises grounds. As they strode along the little-traveled road, bordered by trees, Bud suddenly pointed excitedly. "Isn't that a crow on top of the tree there?"

Tom started. Following Bud's finger, he sighted a

large iridescent black bird on a treetop some distance away.

"Does he belong in a nest or a laboratory?" Tom asked, equally interested. "From here, you couldn't tell the difference," he added, gazing upward. "Except that he's smaller than the mechanical one we've seen so far. But there may be several sizes, for all we know."

"I'll tell you in a few seconds, Tom," Bud whispered.

"What do you mean?"

"Remember I once won second prize in a bird-calling contest in school?"

Tom looked skeptical.

"I'm serious, Tom. Watch this."

Bud threw back his head, cupped his hands to his mouth, and squawked, "Caw, caw, caw!" The crow perked up its head and looked around. Bud cawed again. Now the bird craned its neck trying to locate its fellow creature.

Bud cawed once more and this time the crow called back, scolding angrily.

Tom doubled up with laughter. "You get *first* prize this time, Bud."

After lunch, when the boys were ready to return to Swift Enterprises, Tom told his family what the plans for the afternoon were. His mother begged him not to take any chances and Sandy added impishly:

"Since it's only a crow you're after, I won't invite

myself along. But when you boys are going on a long trip, count me in."

"Okay, Sandy," said Bud. "But we'd have to be sure you wouldn't be a target for remote control before we'd take you." As the girl grimaced, he added, "I'll admit you'd make a swell decoy, though!"

Laughing, Sandy waved good-by to Bud and Tom as they left for the plant. During the two hours remaining before departure, Tom made a careful inspection of all equipment in the Flying Lab. Then he checked to make certain that one of his drone planes was berthed in the *Sky Queen*.

This drone was a lance-nosed, pilotless jet, equipped with a powerful landing forcer that enabled it to capture intruding planes and steer them back by radio control. Tom had used a fleet of these drones to protect his Fearing Island rocket base. Now he intended to use one to capture the crow, if possible, and hoped that his invention had more pulling power than the machinery inside the mysterious mechanical bird.

Next, Tom left to get a portable control panel that gave the small walking robot its orders. After this was set in place in the Flying Lab, the young inventor went to get Walter. To his satisfaction, he noticed a plane flying at great speed high above the plant.

"I hope Flash Ludens was in that plane," Tom murmured, "and that he'll be back."

Hanson met him at the door of his office and they

carried the small walking robot outdoors. Then, in full view, Tom marched him across the grounds to the waiting *Sky Queen*. Walter clumped along awkwardly, while Tom, walking a few steps behind, guided the robot with a small temporary control panel.

Walter was hoisted, head first, through a hatch in the underside of the fuselage and put in a large storage locker. Tom and Bud took their places in the forward pilot's compartment, then taxied the *Sky Queen* to a special quarter-mile square of glazed brick that could withstand the blast of its take-off exhaust.

Tom opened the throttle. With a roar the jet lifters let loose their blast. The great craft shook once and began to lift.

Reaching a good cruising height in the overcast sky, Tom switched off the lifters and sent the forward jets into action. The *Sky Queen* rapidly reached the area where the plane kidnaping had occurred. The sky was deserted.

"Let's cruise around for a while," Bud suggested.

"I'll swing her in a wide circle," said Tom, "so it won't be too obvious that we're playing decoy for that mechanical buzzard."

"Crow," Bud chided.

"Well, it has a buzzard's habits," said Tom. "I wish it would come out of its nest."

The gleaming plane swept back and forth in a lazy circle through the leaden sky for almost an hour without incident. Tom prepared to return to the base.

"That was a wild-crow chase, if I ever saw one," Bud commented.

"I'm afraid so," said Tom, swinging the ship to avoid a large gray cloud. "I think we'll drop under that air smudge."

He reached for the vertical controls.

"Tom!" cried Bud. "Look what's coming out of that cloud! The crow!"

"And it's coming straight at us!" Tom said. "Now for the capture!"

"Watch out, Tom, there are *two* of them this time!"

The second bird was breaking through the cloud and heading for the Flying Lab.

Tom's hands gripped the controls. He shot a glance to the left. Three more black specks were swooping around from the rear, veering clear of the jet exhausts. Another appeared in front of them— then still another.

"They're coming from all sides!" cried Bud. "We're in the middle of a whole flock!"

Tom groaned. This could mean real trouble!

CHAPTER 5

A RARE CAPTURE

AS TOM AND BUD stared anxiously, the mechanical birds darted in and out of the clouds, cutting in front of the *Sky Queen*.

"Three of them are making a pass over the rudder," Bud warned. "What say we run before they ruin the ship?"

"Not yet," said Tom.

The young flier constantly checked the instrument gauges. If they suddenly fluctuated, he would know the mysterious force behind the crows had penetrated the protective coating of Tomasite. Minutes passed with the crows circling and weaving across their flight path, but Tom retained complete control of the Flying Lab. Turning to Bud, he said:

"I didn't think their beamer—or whatever that force is—could get through."

"Good night!" Bud cried. "There's another flock! How many can we hold off?"

"I'm beginning to think that if one crow can't hurt us, neither can a hundred," Tom said confidently.

As the weird parade moved through the threatening skies, the boys watched the strange scene, almost hypnotized.

"What's our next move, Tom?" Bud asked finally. "Do we dare send out the drone?"

"I don't believe so, Bud," Tom replied thoughtfully. "We don't know how strong the crows' force may be, nor how far their operating field extends. Once the drone is outside the hangar, it won't be protected by the *Queen's* Tomasite shielding."

"Hm-m, you've got a point there," Bud said, a vision of the drone falling to its doom crossing his mind. "Drones are valuable equipment."

Tom's mind was working rapidly. In a moment he had the answer. "Bud, there should be a distorter aboard," he said. "If I install it in the drone I'm sure it can resist any beam the crows throw out."

"Swell idea, genius boy. Want me to take over here?"

"No, I'll need your help installing it. Set the *Queen* on the lifters and leave her."

As Tom dashed from the cabin, Bud switched off the forward speed jets, clicked on the lifters so the ship would remain stationary in the air, then followed his friend down the stairs to the storage-inventory closet.

Tom thumbed through a rotary wall file and

quickly located a card with information that a distorter, his own invention, would be found tied down to storage rack number ten. This device was capable of scrambling electrical signals and remote-control beams.

He and Bud carried the instrument to the sliding door that separated the hangar from the rest of the first level. Tom opened it and they clamped the distorter in the sleek drone, connecting the cable to the drone's generator.

Tom started the dynamo and its high, singing screech filled the hangar. Bud felt better already. "Maybe we can nab the whole jet flock." He grinned.

The distorter installed, Bud activated controls releasing the drone's lashing and wheel blocks.

"Prepare to disgorge!" he yelled. "Start her up, skipper!"

Tom pressed the drone's remote-control starter and the hangar doors swung open automatically. A crow shot past the opening, veering to miss the jet stream.

"Set, Bud?" Tom yelled.

"Set! Let's give these mechanized corn feeders a taste of their own medicine!"

Tom threw a switch and for a brief moment the drone's thrust blasted hot gases back through the hangar. Then, with a roar, it leaped forward and careened through space after the marauding crows.

Bud and Tom raced back to the pilot's compartment. "Look at that drone go!" Bud cried, tracking it from the navigation dome's seat.

The powerful little plane whipped in and out of the flock, but the crows seemed to sense its approach and dodged out of the way. Although they managed to avoid the drone for several minutes, whatever was operating them suddenly seemed unable to control the separate maneuvers of the whole flock at once.

"We've caught one!" Bud yelled jubilantly as the drone sucked the bird alongside it. "And another!"

A moment later the rest of the flock flew off at great speed.

"We've got 'em on the run now, Tom!" Bud cried exuberantly. "Let's follow as soon as the drone's berthed."

He dashed back to the hangar while Tom got ready to give the *Sky Queen* the gun.

Tom directed the drone to a reverse blast landing, while Bud manipulated the arresting gear controls from the hangar. When the drone and its two trophies were safely berthed, Bud phoned Tom, who gave the Flying Lab a powerful forward thrust, and the *Sky Queen* soon overtook the crows. The copilot joined his friend.

"I'll follow them for a while," Tom said, slowing his huge ship to match the crows' speed. "Watch for signs of a possible control station."

Bud peered down through binoculars. He spotted familiar landmarks—local farmhouses and factory buildings well known to both boys—but nothing that would suggest a control-station housing.

"These birds will have to lead us somewhere," Tom said.

As if in answer, the entire flock suddenly nose-dived. Tom dropped the *Sky Queen*.

"They're headed for that big open section of Riverton Lake!" Bud yelled.

"They'll probably turn in a second," Tom replied, then gasped incredulously.

In a series of resounding splashes the crows smacked into the water and disappeared.

"Well, how do you like that!" Bud exclaimed in disgust.

Tom switched on the jet lifters and the Lab hovered over the lake.

"Maybe the crows have a water base," Bud suggested.

"I doubt it," said Tom. "Their owner didn't want to reveal his base of operations. We were getting too close for comfort, so he crashed them. He must have a lot more hidden some place, though, or he wouldn't have destroyed so many."

"It was a smart maneuver, all right, sending them to the one place we can't follow," Bud observed.

They crisscrossed the area several times, but failed to find any clues to the hide-out of the owner of the strange missiles.

"We may as well head for home," Tom said. "I

hope that Dilling picked up something." Turning over the controls to Bud, he added, "I'm going down to the hangar and take a look at those crows."

"Good idea," Bud replied. "Let me know what makes those babies tick!"

A few minutes later the buzzer sounded in the pilot's cabin.

"Bud, these crows are fantastic looking at close range," Tom reported. "But I can't see what makes them work without taking them apart. Think I'll wheel one to the physics lab and take a look."

"Roger," Bud said, and pointed the ship toward Shopton.

Yawning and stretching his shoulders, Bud rode the controls lightly. The *Sky Queen*'s smooth flight was relaxing after the afternoon's excitement.

"Wonder what Tom is finding out about those crows," Bud murmured. As he was about to pick up the intercom to find out, an explosion rocked the huge ship!

Bud grabbed for the wheel of the yawing plane with one thought burning in his mind. The explosion must have been in the physics lab!

"Tom!" he yelled in horror. "Tom!"

CHAPTER 6

NARROW ESCAPE

FEARING THE WORST, Bud set the *Sky Queen* on stationary position and hurried toward the laboratory. By this time the ship was filled with an acrid smoke that burned Bud's eyes and made him choke.

He stopped a split second to grab a gas mask from a wall closet, then raced on. His heart pounding in dreaded anticipation, Bud flung open the laboratory door. The huge place, with its many sections, was blanketed with smoke.

Bud dashed from room to room. His friend was not in any of them. Furthermore, it was evident from the little damage in the laboratory that the explosion had not occurred there. But where had it been? And where was Tom?

Heartsick, Bud started down the stairs to the hangar deck. The smoke was thicker here. But through it he could dimly make out another gas-masked figure.

"Tom!" he exclaimed. "Thank goodness! I thought you—"

The muffled sounds reached Tom, who rushed to Bud's side. "I'm okay, Bud. The explosion was in the hangar. It wrecked the sprinkler system. The fire's getting out of control!"

"How about using the bags of sand? We can toss 'em in," Bud suggested.

"No, the fumes are too strong. They'd soon de-activate our mask purifiers."

"What'll we do?" Bud asked, knowing moments of delay were costly. The whole ship might go!

"Get the robot and the control board," Tom replied. "Bring them here. I'm going to the lab for some powerful fire-fighting chemical."

The boys dashed off. Each worked like a demon to accomplish his task. Bud was waiting in the smoky corridor when Tom returned with two fifty-pound cylinders of methyl bromide and a few yards of plastic pressure tubing with a nozzle attached to one end.

"Can you control Walter from behind a closed door?" Bud asked.

"Yes," Tom answered, uncoiling the hose and attaching it to the valve on one of the methyl bromide cylinders. As he began to twist open the cylinder's needle valve, Tom asked Bud to raise one of the robot's arms and tie the nozzle of the hose to it. When everything was ready, Tom jumped to the control panel, saying:

"Open the door, Bud."

Simultaneously one boy pushed a button that controlled the hangar door while the other set the robot in motion. As Walter clumped forward into the hangar, tongues of flame spit from the opening and fierce heat waves rolled into the corridor. Bud closed the door, leaving a crack just wide enough for the hose.

"Here goes the first cylinder," Tom yelled, opening wide the valve. "Get the second one ready, Bud."

Dial needles on the control panel fluctuated wildly as Tom moved the robot through the blazing hangar. When the first cylinder of chemical was used up, Bud quickly uncoupled the hose and transferred to the second.

Within fifteen minutes the robot's valiant battle in the hangar became a victory. The final tongue of flame was snuffed out.

Tom and Bud had to wait until the ship's air conditioning cleared out the fumes before they could remove their masks. When they were able to enter the hangar, the boys could not touch the hot, twisted parts of fused metal that had been the drone plane.

The crow was in minute pieces, scattered about the hangar. Bits of it had pitted the walls and ceiling.

"What do you think caused the explosion, Tom?" Bud asked.

"From the looks of things," Tom answered, "I'd say the crow exploded, taking the drone and almost the entire hangar with it." Suddenly a look of horror crossed his face. "The other crow!" he cried. "It's still in the physics lab. That may explode too!"

Leaping up the stairs two at a time, they dashed into the physics section. The huge mechanical crow was lying on the worktable where Tom had left it, wings outspread and feet sticking up in the air.

"We'd better pitch this thing overboard pronto!" Bud advised, starting to lift it.

"No!" Tom cried. "Don't do that. I'll never be able to learn what's inside."

As Bud gingerly laid the crow back on the worktable, Tom grabbed up a small barrel of oil, poured it into a large tank, and immersed the crow.

"I hope this works," Bud said, not completely sure that the boys would not be blown up, despite Tom's precaution. The metal breastplate of the bird had already been removed, exposing an intricate network of wires and transistors. Now Tom reached for a screw driver and fine pincers. In a moment he had the back of the crow off.

"No bomb here," he muttered.

"What about that bulge in the belly area?" Bud asked nervously.

Tom quickly unbolted a bottom plate. "No," he said. "This is the radio-sensory receiver. The crow sees with its legs. The talons are meshed radar screens—it sort of hears its way along with them."

"That leaves just the head of the bird," said Bud. "Tom, don't you think we'd better quit?"

But Tom, working with delicate precision, had begun to unwind the threading on the sharp-beaked

Tongues of flame spit from the opening

head of the crow. Within was a seepage-diffusion chemical time fuse and a charge of dynamite! But it had been deactivated by the oil.

"Whew!" Bud exclaimed. "You didn't give that old crow a bath a minute too soon! The chemical had eaten along the tape almost to the dynamite!"

Tom admitted being shaken by the whole experience and suggested that they fly back to the plant at once.

Immediately upon their arrival Tom ordered repairs begun on the Flying Lab's hangar, then took the crow to his own metallurgical workshop. Picking up the intercom, he located his father and asked him to come at once to inspect the mechanical bird.

"It's a scientific wonder," he said. "And powerful."

Mr. Swift hurried over and gazed at the crow which Tom had just finished cleaning of oil. After an inspection the elder inventor remarked:

"You're right, Tom. This is a brilliant piece of engineering. It's almost flawless. Not one cubic centimeter of unused space."

"The co-ordinator is an electronic gem of a circuit," Tom added.

His father frowned. "This is the work of a very ingenious scientist. No one else could have planned such a mechanism."

"Yes, Dad. And I'm sure it couldn't be Flash Ludens. He may be an electrical wizard, but he's just a flash in the pan compared to the genius behind this crow!"

"Right," Mr. Swift agreed. "Look at that little gyro which stabilizes the bird in a resting position until it receives directing impulses. Perfect. Absolutely perfect."

"The man must be mad to hobnob with cutthroats like the Briggin gang," Tom said.

"I agree, son. And that makes him all the more dangerous. I want you to take every precaution in tracking him down."

Tom smiled. "I will, Dad," he said. "But I want that relotrol back before he makes some horrible use of my invention."

For a few minutes father and son talked over the improved relotrol on which Tom was working. The new one, to be installed in the control panel inside the atomic energy plant, would be one-hundred-percent radiation proof.

"By the way, Dad," said Tom, "I think I should take a trip out to the plant soon. Do you realize I haven't seen it yet?"

Mr. Swift's eyes twinkled. "It's your own fault," he said good-naturedly. "If you'd stop gallivanting around the world in your own inventions, you might have time to come out West and see my project!"

"You win, Dad." Tom laughed. "I'll go out soon. Hope you'll be there to show me around."

"Wait till you see it, Tom. It's like a white citadel

jutting up out of the wasteland rock desert. In fact, that's what we decided to call it: Citadel. For miles around there's no civilization, just big black boulders and crumbling, eroded pink cliffs."

"Sounds wonderful, Dad. And no chance of harming any neighbors?"

"That's right. The border of the nearest ranch is fifteen miles away." Mr. Swift looked at his watch. "Tom, your poor mother will certainly have every right to chide us for being late to dinner again. It's after eight o'clock. Come on."

The two locked up the laboratory and went at once to Tom's jeep. They drove home quickly and the evening meal was set on the table immediately. But there was no chiding from understanding Mrs. Swift. She was used to serving food at any time of day or night to her adventurous husband and son.

Conversation revolved almost exclusively around the capture of the mechanical crow and its amazing ability, despite its size, to kidnap an object as large as a plane.

Mrs. Swift frowned. "It worries me to think of an ingenious scientist and a bank robber working together. That's a frightening combination for the Swifts to have as enemies."

The conversation was cut short by the insistent buzzing of the videophone from the plant. Tom excused himself and rushed to the screen in the living room. The face that appeared on it was Dilling's. The radioman looked weary and agitated.

"Yes, George," Tom said. "Did you find out anything?"

"Yes. Ham Smith and I took two trucks out. We started work about two hundred miles apart. Each of us picked up the same high-frequency signal shortly after you went up in the Flying Lab, and so did the tower operator at Shopton. We began tracking at once, making a directional fix from each of the three locations. Here's the result."

Dilling held up a large chart before the screen. He had added direction lines and decimal numerical ratings of ascending signal strengths. Using simple triangulation, he had marked in red the point at which all three lines converged. It was about twenty-five miles from Shopton.

"The enemies' control station must be located here," he said.

"I'll go there at once," Tom answered excitedly. "It's almost directly below the spot where the crows first attacked us!"

Switching off the set, he telephoned to Radnor, then Ames and finally Bud at their homes, to meet him in his office at once. He himself went to get the chart. When the four assembled, Tom said:

"I asked you to come here because I didn't want anyone listening in on our phone conversation. We're going on a highly secret mission."

After giving them Dilling's report, Tom outlined his plan for surprising the owners of the crows. "The place may be hard to find and we'll have to go part way on foot," he said. "The spot is some distance from the road. Get flashlights."

They took the black sedan in which Bud had arrived, deciding that the license number of this car would not be known to Tom's mysterious enemies. The last five miles of the trip were rough and progress was slow. It was nearly eleven o'clock before they parked and started through the desolate woods on foot.

Fortunately, there was bright moonlight and use of their flashlights was unnecessary. After walking a quarter of a mile they crossed a small knoll, studded with rocks. Just beyond it stood a stark, lightning-shattered tree. Beside it was a wooden shack.

Tom and his friends dropped to the ground and inched toward it through high weeds.

CHAPTER 7

A MECHANICAL COMEDIAN

TOM, Bud, and the security officers crawled ahead toward the shack. There was not a sound.

A few yards from the dilapidated building, Tom suggested that Harlan and Radnor cover the place from the outside while he and Bud tried the door.

"Flash an S O S if you need any help," Radnor whispered to the boys as they crawled off.

When they reached the shack, Tom and Bud noticed that the door hung open about two feet. Reaching up, Tom rapped lightly on it.

Silence!

"Guess there's nobody home!" Bud chuckled softly.

"I'll go first," Tom whispered. Beaming his flashlight, he got to his feet, crouched over, and began inching into the shack. Suddenly the door swung wide with a shrill squeak. Tom jumped back.

55

Then, realizing that a gust of wind had moved the door, he started forward again, tiptoeing into the one-room structure. Bud followed and both boys played their powerful flashlights around. The beams revealed only cobwebs and emptiness.

"Guess we came to the wrong place," Bud said.

"I don't think so," Tom replied. He had been pivoting his flashlight around the room, probing into corners and searching the roofing beams. "What's that up there?" He aimed his light overhead.

Dangling by a wire from a crossbeam was a large white cardboard sign. On it was crudely printed:

WE EXPECTED YOU, TOM SWIFT JR.

The young inventor gasped, partly in fury, partly in disbelief. "But how—" he asked, puzzled. "How could anyone have learned we were coming here? You know how careful we were about planning this raid in secret!"

Bud stared in bewilderment, then flashed for Radnor and Ames. When they entered, he pointed to the swinging sign.

"So they beat us to the draw," Harlan said in disgust. He walked over and studied the message. "It was placed here within the hour, Tom. The ink on the printing is still wet enough to smear."

"But how did your enemies find out our strategy, Tom?" said Radnor. "It seems incredible."

"They couldn't have tapped the videophone lines," Tom said. "The signals are sent scrambled, modulated against random noise. Only our own receivers have built-in decoding records. And certainly no one was spying on my home," he added. "No signal sounded to show anyone tried to cross the magnetized zone around the house."

"That," said Ames, "leaves only the plant. There must have been a security leak at Swift Enterprises, sometime within the past two hours. It's the only other way our plans could have become known so quickly and thoroughly."

"Everyone at the plant has been double-checked," Radnor spoke up. "And there were no visitors after four o'clock. I can't understand a slip-up like this."

Harlan Ames began to pace the floor of the shack. "We'll run another check," he said. "Tomorrow we'll put a tracer through on second cousins and casual outside friends of the friends of employees, if necessary. Somewhere we'll find the leak and then—"

Suddenly Ames leaped into the air, yelling, "Ouch! My foot! I just jabbed it on something sharp."

As Tom focused the beam of his flashlight on the floor, Ames hopped around on one foot, clutching the other with his hand.

"Went right through the sole of my shoe," he said.

"Here's what you stepped on," said Tom. A sharp metal point was sticking out of the floor boards.

"Watch it, Tom," cautioned Bud. "This may be a scheme to accomplish what the crows were supposed to do. We never thought of checking the cellar!"

Tom motioned the others to back away while he probed at the surrounding boards. "I think that this metal is attached to something underneath. Doesn't look like a bomb from here."

Bud, Radnor, and Ames helped him wrench loose more of the flooring. Below was a shallow cellar, containing a unit of gears and motors.

"Well, that couldn't be what manipulated those crows," Bud said.

"No," Tom agreed. "I have an idea the control unit was probably mobile—maybe built into big vans—and that's how they managed to clear out so soon."

Tom studied the large mechanism after Radnor and Ames lifted it from the cellar. "This looks like a timing control of some sort. I've seen only one other like it. That was in the door of a bank safe! I'll bet that this is a duplicate of a vault's timing mechanism and someone was using it to experiment with."

The others stared at him. "Flash Ludens?" they chorused.

"That's my guess," Tom nodded. "Let's take this along."

Outside the shack, Bud's flashlight beam showed large, deep tire tracks. Pointing them out to Tom, he said, "These prove your theory about a mobile control unit, all right."

The four carried the timing device to their sedan and started for Shopton. On the way back, Ames used the car's first-aid kit to treat his foot. During a lull in the conversation, Tom flipped on the radio to get the news.

"—and here is a flash just in," said the announcer presently. "There has been a daring robbery at the Farmington National Bank. The police have not given out any details as yet. They merely said that an unusual method was used. The night watchman, who was knocked out, reported the robbery when he revived. As soon as there is more news, this station—"

"I'll bet it was the Briggin gang!" Bud declared.

"And I have a hunch how the robbery was carried out," Tom said. "We'll stop at the Farmington police station and show the captain that gimmick in the back seat. I'm sure it's a clue."

The young inventor explained that a small machine to change the time set on the vault could have been smuggled into the bank by an accomplice working as a clerk or messenger. Inserted in the timer, it could change the hour at which the safe would open.

"Then the gang just walked in and cleaned out the money," said Bud.

"Yes," Tom replied, "that device would make the job a push-over."

"Do you think Flash Ludens' genius friend figured out the gimmick by experimenting on the timer we have with us?" Radnor asked.

"I'd say so," Tom answered, turning down a side road that led to Farmington.

Upon reaching police headquarters there, he found the place in an uproar. All off-duty policemen had been called in and the captain was issuing orders to them in a clipped, authoritative tone.

Tom waited until the excitement died down, then he introduced himself and asked for a private interview with Captain English. Tom told as much of the story as he could without revealing his own special interest in the Briggin gang. After examining the device which the others carried in, the police officer exclaimed:

"You've figured this out all right, Tom. The bank safe had the same kind of time-lock system as this one you found. The department's certainly grateful to you." As Tom arose to leave, the captain added with a grim smile, "Now if you'll nab the robbers themselves, we'll strike off a medal for you!"

The young inventor went home for a much-needed sleep. He was late for breakfast the next morning, but his mother, Sandy, and their friend Phyllis Newton were enjoying cocoa and doughnuts and having a lively discussion.

"Good morning," Tom said, kissing his mother and giving each of the girls an affectionate pat on the shoulder. "Hi, Phyl? How's tricks?"

"Tricks are bad, Tom. That's why I'm here. You're just the person to save the day."

Tom sat down, dug a spoon into half a grapefruit, and grinned. "Phyl, you're making a hero out of me even before I know why. What's the story?"

Phyl, a pretty girl, with dark hair and large brown eyes, was the daughter of Mr. Swift's lifelong friend

Ned Newton, who now managed the old Swift Construction Company. She was always Tom's date on parties, and Sandy and Bud often went along. Sometimes the four young people would go off together on scientific treks. Sandy was an excellent pilot, and Phyl had a flare for sketching which many times had come in handy.

"It has to do with the entertainment tomorrow night," Phyl explained. "You remember, the big one to raise money for the hospital?" Tom nodded. He recalled that the girls were on the fund committee. "Well, our best act has been washed up. We've got to substitute something in a hurry. It's against the rules to engage a professional—only amateurs can be in it."

Tom gave the girl a long look. "You're not hinting that I become a song-and-dance man, I hope!"

Phyl laughed. "Not you, but one of your robots," she replied.

The young inventor stared in disbelief. "What! Why, Phyl, that would mean a major operation on the robot's interior. He'd have to be remote controlled and it would take hours and hours of—"

"Tom," Mrs. Swift spoke up, "is what Phyl's asking an impossibility?"

"No, but—"

"If you worked at it today and tomorrow, with Bud and others helping, you could do it?"

"Yes, Mother. But—"

"Then I want you to do it," Mrs. Swift said. "So

far as I know, you've never used your scientific talents for charitable purposes." She smiled. "Unless your turning criminals over to the authorities without reward could be called working for humanity. Tom, I'd like you to do your share for the show tomorrow night."

"All right, Mother. I'll do it. But I'll need Sandy's and Phyl's help."

"Wonderful!" the two girls cried. "When do we start?"

"Come down to the lab at three tomorrow afternoon. We'll have the robot ready by then."

All day and the next morning Tom, Bud, and three engineers worked to perfect a portable control panel, inserting tapes to send messages to a six-foot-tall robot so that he could walk, dance, and sing. Record after record was tried and discarded before the mechanical man's steps synchronized with the music.

In the meantime, Arvid Hanson had been working on the head to make it look more presentable to an audience. By the time Sandy and Phyl arrived, the robot appeared as a deadpan, comical-faced creature whose eyes roved from side to side.

"Meet Herbert," Tom said. As the girls giggled, the robot bowed stiffly. "I'll give you a demonstration," the young inventor went on, "then show you just how to work these dials. It's as simple as running a record player."

Herbert went through his performance perfectly,

to the delight of the girls, then both worked the dials, doing a satisfactory job. The four young people had an early supper at the Enterprises plant and at six thirty left for the armory where the entertainment was to take place.

By eight o'clock the auditorium was filled and the show began. Since the robot performance was to be the last number, Tom and Bud remained behind the scenes, carefully guarding the canvas-covered figure and the control panel until the curtain rang down on the preceding act.

Then the boys wheeled the robot to the center of the stage and took off the cover. Tom quickly reviewed the instructions for operating Herbert and turned the panel over to the girls. Then he and Bud took their places in the center of the second row in the audience.

Bud was smiling because he and another engineer had secretly made a few additions to the mechanical man. They had rigged up a secondary signal receiver that cut into the robot's main circuit. In Bud's pocket was a miniature control panel. When the girls finished their show, he planned to make the robot do a few tricks that were not on the program.

The master of ceremonies walked out. "And now," he said, chuckling, "we present a surprise number in place of the one on your program. World-renowned vaudeville trio: Swift, Newton—and Herbert the Robot."

The band struck up "Yankee Doodle." The cur-

tains parted and an amber spotlight revealed the in-
animate Herbert standing between the two girls.
They all bowed and the mechanical man lighted up
in several places. As the audience broke into applause, the girls hurried to the wings to take over
the controls.

Herbert began to jig across the stage. The crowd
broke into uproarious laughter. As the girls worked
the regulating dials, the robot launched into a series
of disjointed acrobatics. His lights blinked on and
off, and his big eyes rolled from side to side. The applause was deafening.

"Now we'll make him sing," said Sandy, and
turned on the tape for this part of the act.

Herbert's voice was surprisingly like that of a famous crooner, making the audience laugh all the
louder as the robot imitated the singer's well-known
gestures.

Amid tremendous hand clapping the curtain went
down. Then, as it arose again for a second bow from
Herbert, Bud clicked a knob in his pocket panel.
The robot walked to the front of the stage and
stumped down the steps toward the audience. Bud's
plan was to give people in the first row a little scare,
then stop Herbert just as he reached them.

As he drew closer, the humanoid machine looked
menacing. Had he gone out of control? the audience
wondered. Would he harm someone?

"Oh!" cried a girl in the front row, shrinking back
in her seat.

Bud decided that the time had come to end his joke. He turned the knob that would cause Herbert to reverse and march back up the steps to the stage.

But, to the boy's consternation, Herbert continued to advance. Something had gone wrong!

CHAPTER 8

A SUSPICIOUS OFFER

PANICKY, Bud threw the "off" switch of the control panel in his pocket to halt the robot's rampage. But Herbert continued to advance menacingly toward the audience.

"Tom!" Bud cried. "Let me get past! I've got to stop him!"

By this time, Herbert, arms stretched before him, was stalking for the side of the hall, where town officials were seated. The robot headed directly for the mayor of Shopton!

Bud was frantic. "Tom, do something!" he. pleaded.

"Okay."

To Bud's amazement, his friend did not seem to be the least bit upset. Abruptly Herbert stopped, took a bow, then turned back and calmly sauntered in his awkward way up the stage steps. Here he bowed again, then walked to the wings, with the audience going into thunderous applause.

Tom hurried backstage with Bud at his heels. Sandy and Phyl stood speechless. "Wh-what happened?" they finally cried together.

Bud was about to confess his part when Tom replied, "Didn't you like it? Bud and I thought we'd have some fun. We both had small control panels in our pockets for Herbert's extra-surprise act."

"Well, I think you might have told us," said Sandy, while Bud's jaw dropped open in amazement. He realized now that Tom had discovered the additional tape he and the engineer had rigged up in the robot and had installed one of his own!

The robot headed directly for the mayor

"The joke's on me," Bud admitted.

"That's what you get," Phyl said archly, "for trying to put one over on Tom Swift!"

"Sh!" someone called. "The finale is going on!"

Everyone remained quiet while the chorus went through their last number. Then Tom said, "We'll take Herbert back to the lab and go on to the party from there." The foursome were joining a group of the entertainers at the home of one of the girls.

"Pardon me, please," said a voice behind them. The group turned to face a tall man with a thin black mustache. He was dressed in evening clothes, although none of the other men in the audience had been.

"How do you do?" he said in a theatrical and affected voice. "I am Tsorka, a traveling magician. I was passing through this town when I heard of the benefit performance and decided to attend. Very fine. Very fine. But your unusual act, young ladies, was by far the best. Your robot is magnificent. Beside it, even my shredded umbrella restoration is a pale trick. I must have your mechanical man for my act."

"He's not for sale," Tom said coolly.

"I am prepared to pay a rental fee of one thousand dollars a month for the use of your robot," Tsorka went on.

Tom was taken aback by the unexpected offer. "I'm sorry," he replied. "Herbert belongs to me and is not for rent. He's only an experimental model and could easily go berserk. I couldn't take the risk."

The man drew himself up indignantly. "Now look here, sir. I've made a very liberal offer. Be reasonable. I'm sure we can come to terms. I'm prepared to pay you right here and now."

Instinctively Bud moved over in front of the robot. People did not ordinarily carry a thousand dollars around with them.

Tom, equally suspicious, wondered if Tsorka could be one of his mysterious enemies. Smiling, he said:

"I'm sure, Mr. Tsorka, you could learn to run a robot with a few lessons. I'll be glad to design one to do stage specialty tricks for you. Where can I get in touch with you?"

The man's dark eyes glittered. "Very well," he said. "I rarely remain in the same city long. However, I'll be back in this vicinity in two days. I'll phone you then."

He turned and left. Sandy and Phyl protested to Tom that he should have nothing to do with the stranger.

Bud agreed. "I think he's a phony."

"Right," said Tom. "But one worth learning more about."

The young people deliberated awhile and decided to be very watchful to ensure Herbert's safe return to the plant. The boys directed the robot into the back of the truck, then Bud climbed in. The girls sat in the cab with Tom. He eased the truck out of the armory driveway and drove slowly through town.

Then, reaching open country, Tom headed for Swift Enterprises.

Bud was nervous. He called, "I think a pair of headlights are hanging onto us rather close, Tom."

In the reflector mirror the young inventor caught a glimpse of bright headlights swinging along the road behind them.

"This courier truck can beat him," Tom said grimly, giving it more speed. But the trailing car seemed to be gaining on them. Tom instructed the girls to keep down and told Bud to warn him if it got any closer or attempted to cut them off.

"Got you, chum," said Bud. "But watch the curve at the cloverleaf."

Tom made the turn neatly, but the tires of the car that seemed to be tailing them turned with reckless squeals.

Swinging off the ramp, Tom took a short cut to the plant. When the other car did the same thing, there was no longer any doubt in Tom's mind that its driver was purposely following them.

With a final burst of speed he shot toward the rear entrance to the plant. The truck's special beamer activated the gate's electronic eye, and as the barrier opened just ahead of them, the vehicle raced through. The solid gate slammed shut instantly. They heard the screech of tires as the car behind turned abruptly and raced off.

"Thank goodness!" said Phyl. "Here's hoping I never have to ride with Herbert again!"

The tension over, everyone laughed. Tom drove the truck directly to the modelmaking division and the young people alighted.

"As soon as we put Herbert to bed," Bud remarked, "we'll go to the party."

The evening's gay festivities helped Tom to forget the strange chase to the plant. But later that night, recalling the incident, he began to think about the advisability of having not one but two giant robots. Then if anything happened to the one now nearly complete, he would have another to take its place. The following morning he started to work on a second giant robot. This one would run on a different frequency as a double precaution. As soon as work on it was well under way, the young inventor turned his attention to the problem of constructing a new relotrol. During the following two days he discarded one idea after another. Hard at work in his laboratory, Tom became so absorbed that eating and sleeping were almost forgotten.

Chow was worried. "That young genius sure burns himself up like a roarin' prairie fire," he said to himself, gazing fondly at the youth who sat at a drawing board, a plastic-hooded shade over his eyes. "Brand my mashed mongoose fritters, I jest got to make him eat. . . . Tom," he said aloud.

Tom looked up from his workbench. "I wonder if a high-frequency band-pass filter would work?" he was thinking aloud.

Chow sighed. "You ain't payin' a coyote's-sized

attention to me," he complained. The cook scratched at the stubble of his beard and squinted into the glare of the table lamp. "What you tryin' to do, Tom?"

A voice from the doorway answered. It was Bud Barclay with a cup of hot chocolate from the cafeteria.

"It's simple, Chow. Our master electrician here is perfecting a method to stifle random noise."

"Meanin' me?" Chow looked downcast.

"No, Chow," Bud replied, grinning. Trying to imitate Tom's method of explanation, he said, "These are electrical noises built up by cascades of amplifiers used in making analogues of the robot's work problems. They disturb the signals. Then when radiation is added—"

"Hey! I think I've hit it!" Tom announced. "The next relotrol will be operated by frequency modulation, just like FM radios. The signals will have nothing in common with radiation and the robot won't be confused."

"Swell!" said Bud. "Now maybe you'll tell Chow we both need something substantial to eat—even mongoose fritters."

"What!" cried the cook in disbelief. "Well, I'll rustle up some Texas grub pronto."

Just then the telephone rang. Chow picked it up.

"Tom," he said, after listening for a moment, "Radnor says he's got some important news for you!"

CHAPTER 9

TELLTALE X-RAY

"HELLO, Rad. What's the big news?" Tom asked.

The head of security police spoke rapidly. "We have the leak traced down to one trickle, Tom. Ames and the staff really worked overtime on this one. They went back through miles of microfilm records, first of Enterprises and then all the way into the earliest employment files of the old Swift Construction Company."

"And you dug up something vital?" Tom asked eagerly.

"Nothing from the records," Radnor replied. "But we did learn that a worker in the division where the robot skeletons are fused vanished from town yesterday without any explanation. We're checking on buddies he might have had at the Enterprises plant and also trying to trace his movements."

"Anything I can do to help?" Tom asked.

73

"Not yet," Radnor answered. "But we'll let you know. And we'll keep you informed of our progress."

He hung up and Tom relayed the message to Bud. "It looks bad," Bud remarked. "No telling what secrets have gone to your enemies."

Tom was as much disturbed at the thought of disloyalty on the part of an employee as he was by the fact that some of his inventions were being given to outsiders before he could patent them. Not of a suspicious nature, Tom liked to feel that after a new worker had once been screened he could be trusted implicitly.

It was late evening before Tom was able to shake off his depressed mood. He, Bud, Phyl, and Sandy were in the Swift living room. They had just finished talking about the latest hit records when Sandy said:

"Tom, Phyl and I have a wonderful idea—"

"No more robot entertainments!" Tom protested, laughing.

"This is something very different. You're going out to the new atomic energy plant soon. We thought—"

Sandy stopped speaking because the house alarm had suddenly started buzzing. This meant that the protective magnetic field surrounding the Swift home had been activated by the arrival of an unexpected visitor.

Tom leaped from his chair and dashed to the front door. Bud followed. Both glanced at a dial which registered in degrees the amount of metal on visitors, enabling the Swifts to detect any concealed weapons.

"He hasn't much on him," Tom whispered as the bell rang. "About enough to account for keys, watch, and dental work."

Tom opened the door. A short, rather squat man stood in the outer vestibule. His hair, though dark, was streaked with gray and his complexion was ruddy.

"Tom Swift Jr.?"

"Yes," replied Tom questioningly. "And this is my friend Bud Barclay. Will you come in?"

The man stepped into the hall. "My name's Shanzer," he began. "I'm an engineer with the Trutype Safe Company."

"Offhand, I can't remember ever hearing of your firm, Mr. Shanzer."

"We are rather new in the field," the caller said. "But Trutype knows you. We understand from one of our men who attended a performance here that your company is building some rather impressive robots. We want to commission you to devise one especially for us."

Tom studied the man carefully. Something about him seemed vaguely familiar. Yet Tom could not remember encountering him before. His name? No, he had never heard of anyone named Shanzer. Had he seen a picture of him, perhaps?

Like a flash a scene came to Tom of Ames, in the Swifts' office, uncurling a photograph between his thumb and forefinger. Pins Zoltan! Could this be the bank robber?

Tom offered Shanzer a chair, all the while studying the man. His height seemed to fit Pin's description. True, the hair color was different. Pins was supposed to be a blond, but he could have dyed his hair.

Tom had to be certain. Somehow he must let Bud know of his suspicions and then prove them, one way or another. Tom decided to use the baseball code the boys had devised some time ago to warn each other of impending danger.

"It seems to me that a robot might fit nicely into a business like yours," Tom said. "I could design one that would not only lift heavy safes weighing many tons, but at the same time would be equipped with a set of thin metal grippers with tips more sensitive than those on human fingers. In an emergency it could feel the tumblers and open a safe where the combination had been lost."

Shanzer beamed. "Just what we want," he said.

"Yes, we'd like to *play ball* with you, Mr. Shanzer," Tom continued.

Bud stiffened alertly at the code signal. He shot a glance at Tom and received a verifying nod. The signals were on!

"Suppose the three of us go over to my lab," Tom said, "and take a look at the various kinds now being developed. In that way, Mr. Shanzer, you could choose exactly those features you want combined in your robot."

Shanzer agreed, then looked inquiringly at Bud. Tom quickly explained that Bud worked with him on the robot project.

Bud in turn gave his friend a puzzled look. If he were suspicious of the visitor, why was he inviting him to the plant? But Tom seemed to know what he was doing.

After their arrival at the laboratory building, it soon became obvious to Bud that Tom was not giving away any secrets. He led them through only nonsecurity areas. As they entered a more specialized section, Bud realized that Tom was steering the unsuspecting visitor toward the small but powerful X-ray machine which Tom had built to help him in his research, and which was always kept loaded with photographic plates.

Bud, on the pretext of illuminating the robot laboratory, went ahead and unobtrusively switched on the apparatus.

"While Bud is lighting up the shop, perhaps you'd be interested in this map showing our layout here," Tom suggested to the suspect, who had now been maneuvered to a position in front of the X-ray machine.

Actually the map contained nothing of vital importance, but while Shanzer looked at it, Tom explained a few minor and well-known functions of the assembly-line technique used at the plant. At the same time, several different exposures were being taken of Shanzer.

Tom and Shanzer continued their walk down the corridor. Bud waited to remove and examine the X-ray photographs which had been automatically developed by the machine, and then hastened to rejoin them at the corner.

"Well, Mr. Shanzer," he said, "what do you think of this place? Personally, I feel that when the Swifts built it they were just about *batting a thousand.*"

The code phrase for *guilty!*

CHAPTER 10

DEAD-END TRAIL

TOM UNDERSTOOD the signal perfectly. It meant that Bud had detected something in the X-rays that made him suspect the visitor. Was it surgical pins in his spine?

Before proceeding further, Tom determined to get a look at the X-rays. As they walked on, Bud slipped one of the X-ray photographs into his hand. Dropping behind, Tom held it up to a light. There was no doubt about it. The man they were escorting was Pins Zoltan!

"He'll probably make a violent denial when I accuse him," Tom thought. "And I can't fight him with that infirmity of his. I'll let the police handle him."

Continuing down the corridor, Tom maneuvered his visitor and Bud toward a hall that ended at a locked supply room, then Tom pressed a button on a nearby panel. A fire door dropped with a bang behind them, sealing off the corridor and isolating the three of them from the rest of the building.

"What's happening?" demanded Zoltan, turning around. "Where did that panel come from?"

Zoltan backed toward the fire door

Though tense, Bud gave a forced laugh. "Tom, somebody dropped the ball after the third strike!"

"What ball?" the visitor yelled. "What's the matter with you guys? Are you talking in riddles?"

"From the looks of things," Tom remarked calmly, "it seems the runner was caught off base."

"Caught? What?"

The boys sprang into action. Tom went toward Zoltan as Bud grabbed for a wall telephone. The man backed toward the fire door.

"No use, Pins," said Tom. "We know who you are and right now you're cornered. There's no place for you to run. This door doesn't go up until the police are on the other side. They'll come as soon as I give Bud the signal to call them." Tom paused. "But first, I want a few facts from you."

Zoltan leered contemptuously. "You'll learn nothing from me! You've got the wrong man. My name's Shan—"

"Come on, Pins. We took an X-ray of you." He showed Zoltan the photograph. "You can't escape. Now, tell me, who is the mastermind behind this move against us?"

Pins remained silent, glaring in hatred.

"Word got around that you and your gang had given up bank robbing," Bud put in, "but you pulled a beaut the other night."

"Who said so?" Zoltan demanded.

Bud did not answer. Instead Tom said, "What does the Briggin gang plan to do with my invention that they stole?"

Zoltan snarled and backed up to the fire door.

"Come on, Pins. Open up! Science once saved your life. What have you got against it?" Tom demanded.

"I'm not telling you anything, Tom Swift!"

Zoltan slid along the fire door, feeling for the control button. His shifty eyes had a look of desperation. As Pins neared the release mechanism, Tom lunged toward him. But he was too late. The door zipped up like a window shade suddenly released. Zoltan fell to the floor and rolled into the corridor.

"Oh, my back!" he screamed in pain.

Tom, moved by pity, ran to the crumpled figure. Bud barked an alert through the phone, asking for plant police and a stretcher. The guards arrived within two minutes.

Zoltan still lay on the floor, having refused first aid from Tom. Hatred blazed in his eyes.

"Take him to Shopton Hospital," Tom told the men. "I'll send the town police there."

As two of the guards lifted Pins to the stretcher, he screamed fanatically, "They'll get you, Tom Swift! The rest of the gang will get you!" He vanished into an elevator, flanked by his guards.

Bud mopped his forehead. "Tom, I'm scared," he said. "I've never seen such hatred on any man's face. When the Briggin gang hears what happened, your life will certainly be in danger."

"Don't worry," said Tom. "I've been in worse jams."

Nevertheless, the young inventor was worried as he and Bud drove to the Swift home. By morning, however, in the familiar surroundings of his own office, Tom regained his natural optimism. He had an early appointment with Phil Radnor to talk over again the possibility of a security leak among employees.

Tom sat staring into space, thinking out the problem of combating the effects of radiation on the giant robot's television-camera eyes. He looked at the large silver model of the Flying Lab which stood on one corner of his desk. So absorbed was Tom, though, that actually he was paying no attention to it.

A sudden thud brought him back to reality. Radnor had dropped a stack of folders on the desk.

"Good morning," he said. "Well, here they are— all of them. Two thousand man hours of work, all for nothing. And no sooner do we finish our check than the disappearing worker returns. He'd taken time off—of all things—to elope! Had a leave coming to him, so he just up and took it." As Tom grinned, Radnor concluded, "The fellow had nothing to do with an information leak. Completely innocent."

"Then we're back where we started." Tom sighed.

"Right," said the security man. "A false lead all the way. We'll just have to begin tracing new suspects. Well, I'll be on my way."

His exit coincided with the arrival of Sandy Swift and they chatted for a few minutes. After the security officer left, she perched on the edge of her brother's desk.

"Tom," she said, "we were interrupted last night when I was telling you about my wonderful idea." Sandy smiled, then continued, "How about taking Bud and Phyl and me along when you go out to the atomic energy plant?"

"I'm afraid not, Sis. Sorry. You wouldn't be allowed inside." Tom reminded her of the strict security regulations, as well as the constant danger of exposure to radiation.

"I wouldn't want to go inside all that concrete, anyway," said Sandy. "Neither would Phyllis. So that's all right. We just want to see the interesting country around there.

"It's pretty barren," her brother said.

"I know that, Tom. Ever since Dad started the plant in co-operation with the government, I've been studying about the history and people of that area."

"The Indians, you mean?" Tom asked.

"Yes. There's a tribe not many miles from the plant. Phyl and Bud and I could spend our time visiting them and learning more about their customs."

"It sounds okay so far," Tom said.

His sister went on in a coaxing tone. "In fact, there's a vague old Indian legend about a buried tribal treasure on top of Purple Mesa, a lonely, jagged-edged plateau not far from the Citadel."

"Why hasn't the treasure been removed if it really exists?"

"Nobody's been up there because the sides of the plateau have been cut and eroded by sandstorms. They're too steep for climbing."

"And you think we should investigate the legend?"

Tom asked, a twinkle in his eye. "I suppose we could always use some extra gold."

"Stop teasing," said Sandy. "The story might be true. Tom, we could drop down on the flat top of the mesa by helicopter."

"You certainly make it sound exciting," her brother conceded. "Tell you what. If Mother says okay, we'll do it."

"Thanks. I'll ask her and the others right away. When do we leave?"

"I still have work to do on the robots. And the *Sky Queen* repairs haven't been completed yet." Then he laughed. "But cheer up, Sandy, we'll go as soon as possible."

As Sandy left, Tom reached for the phone and contacted the underground hangar. He spoke to the foreman.

"Do you think that the rest of the bent interior ribs can be torn out and new ones fabricated in half the time listed on the original work order?" Tom asked.

He was told that only the spraying of Tomasite might cause some delay.

"I'll have a couple of engineers from the high-polymer pilot plant come over to take care of that," Tom promised.

"Then we'll have the *Queen* ready in half the time," the foreman assured him.

An hour later Sandy called back to report that

both Mrs. Swift and Mrs. Newton had given consent to their daughters' making the trip. Bud took the news of the impending jaunt with enthusiasm.

"I sure could use some of your buried gold, you old mesa pirate," he said, settling in a chair in Tom's office.

Tom laughed. "I'll give you half of all we dig up, brother buccaneer."

Presently the boys settled down to sober conversation. Bud had brought news that Pins Zoltan was greatly improved physically, but he was still sullen and uncommunicative. Nothing had been heard from the magician.

"We're getting nowhere solving the mystery of the crows and the stolen relotrol," he said.

"Maybe the gang has given up," Tom suggested.

"Don't be too sure," his friend advised. "By the way, are there any newfangled security methods being used at the Citadel?"

"No, but Dad and I decided to set up a drone aircraft protective covering over the plant," Tom told him. "With an air umbrella, we'll feel a lot safer about all the secret equipment and the power housing. I'm taking a drone plane along on our trip for a test run."

"Radio control should prove simple in that wide-open country," Bud remarked. "Well, I'm off to put the *Skeeter* through its paces, to be sure it's in good shape to go hunting for that Injun gold!"

Bud went off to test the *Sky Queen's* helicopter

and Tom did not see him again that day. The next morning Tom decided to walk to work. The sun was shining and he whistled happily as he took the back way through woods, across a stream, and onto an open road that led to the Enterprises grounds.

Suddenly Tom was conscious of a whirring sound in the air directly above him. Looking up, he found himself gazing into the poised talons of a mechanical crow that was swooping down upon him!

Tom dodged to one side of the road, just barely missing the bird's talons. He started to run, but his legs were no match for the crow's speed. Tom zigzagged like a broken-field runner eluding a football tackler, but the crow followed his every move.

Once its wings hit him a glancing blow on the shoulder. Tom winced, rolled to the ground, and sprang to his feet again. The crow's talons cut a gash in his scalp. Tom grabbed the crow's left leg, but a second later it wrenched itself loose.

"So this is Zoltan's revenge," Tom thought, glancing wildly about for help. The road was deserted.

Silently the crow dived again. Then, leveling off, its right wing hit the base of Tom's skull. He toppled over, unconscious.

CHAPTER 11

STEEL SINEWS

AT TOM'S OFFICE in Swift Enterprises there was confusion and consternation. Videophone, telephone, and short-wave radio calls were coming in one after another. To each Miss Trent would answer, "Tom is not here." Sighing, she would reply to another.

"Central Seaboard, calling Tom Swift. Central Seaboard—" The same answer.

"Elheimer, West Coast . . . do you read me? Do you read me?"

"Call back later."

"Rick Dalton to Swift Enterprises. Come in, Swift."

The trunk lines tangled and crossed. Buzzers rang incessantly throughout the main building, in the underground hangar, at all the testing laboratories in a search for the young inventor, but he could not be found.

"I've never seen anything like it," said Miss Trent to Marco, the elderly night watchman for the section. He was late going off duty. "It isn't young Mr. Swift's way of doing things. He doesn't place advance calls and not arrive to receive them. What could have happened?"

Marco frowned and shrugged as the secretary took a long-distance call from Tom's father, who was phoning from the atomic energy plant.

"No, Mr. Swift, Tom hasn't been in touch with the house since he left some time ago. I've tried there twice. They say he started out as usual. Just a minute, Mr. Swift. Here comes Bud Barclay."

Bud picked up an extension phone. "Hello, Mr. Swift. Sorry, but we haven't located Tom yet. I've been searching the buildings and grounds. Sandy says he left for the plant over two hours ago. As soon as he arrives, I'll have him call you."

"I don't like this, Bud," Mr. Swift said, deep concern in his voice. "Call the house again. If Tom hasn't established contact, take out the bloodhounds and get on his trail."

"Right, sir," Bud promised, hanging up. He checked the Swift home again, but Tom had not called. Bud told Miss Trent the plan and hurried off.

Behind the Swift home were kennels which held Sandy's two prize bloodhounds. The dogs had already proven their worth in tracking down a few criminals.

In a moment Bud and Sandy had fitted long leather leashes to the collars of the hounds and were ready to start out. Sandy held a jacket of Tom's for the dogs to sniff, then she and Bud gave them full leash. The floppy-eared dogs yelped anxiously and tugged their masters along behind them.

Out the drive, across the road, and into the woods they ran with Bud and Sandy stumbling over rocks and logs. The trail led down the Stony Brook bridle path, across the main highway, back into the woods again.

"Tom sure took the back way!" Bud exclaimed, as the animals guided them. They raced over the route Tom had taken, until they reached a shallow stream. There the dogs stopped and howled.

"Oh, oh!" cried Sandy. "They've lost the scent at the water."

"We'll lead them over to the other side," said Bud. "I think Tom leaped from stone to stone. Too bad they're wet. The scent's gone."

As the dogs splashed through the water, Sandy and Bud jumped across on the stones. Reaching the far side, Bud's bloodhound gave a yank that almost pulled him over.

"They've found the scent again!" exclaimed Sandy.

The animals dashed through the woods, across a field, and down the road. Suddenly they began zigzagging off and on the road.

"The dogs are going crazy!" Bud cried.

At that moment Sandy's bloodhound pulled the leash from her hand and raced ahead. A few seconds later he stopped at a ditch in a field and began to bay.

Bud and Sandy ran up. "It's Tom!" cried Bud. "He's in the ditch!"

"Oh!" Sandy took one look at her brother's still form, sprawled face down, and gulped. Was he—?

Bud felt his friend's pulse. "He's still alive, Sandy!" He checked for broken bones. Finding none, he lifted Tom gently and carried him to a grassy rise.

"Oh, look at those cuts and that swelling on his head!" said Sandy, horrified. She dipped her handkerchief in a nearby stream and held it against Tom's forehead. In a few minutes the young inventor stirred and blinked.

"Oh-h-h! The crow! It's—it's after me. Can't—"

"Wake up, Tom! It's Bud. I'm no crow."

Tom shook his head to clear his vision. Then he opened his eyes wide. "What— Sandy, Bud, where did you come from?" he mumbled. "And where am I?"

"The bloodhounds found you here," Sandy explained. "When you didn't show up at the plant, we became worried and started a search. What happened, Tom?"

Her brother related the attack by the crow.

"What!" his listeners cried unbelievingly, and

Sandy added, "You're very lucky, Tom. If that crow hadn't leveled off after its dive, you might not be alive now and talking to us."

"I guess you're right." Tom grinned weakly.

"I'd like to bet," said Bud, "that whoever sent it probably thought the bird had killed you."

"No doubt," Tom groaned, clutching his head.

"We must get you home at once, Tom," said Sandy. "We can talk later."

While Tom was at home recuperating that day, George Dilling and Bud, incensed at this attempt on their friend's life, set out to scour the countryside. They combed every farmhouse and barn, looking in wells, tanks, and silos for a possible base of operations and the person behind the attack.

No clues were found. They returned, angered by their failure, but resolved to track down the scoundrel sooner or later.

Tom, after hearing the results of the search, commented, "The crow's movements must have been controlled from a plane or a truck, although I didn't notice any."

"You're probably right, Tom," Bud agreed.

The next morning Tom insisted he felt well enough to return to work. When Mrs. Swift protested, he said:

"I can't afford to hold up work on the giant robot just because of a few bird scratches. Dad is depending on me."

"One thing you must promise me," she said.

"What's that, Mother?"

"Not to make the trip out West until you're completely well."

"All right, I promise."

Eager to make every minute count, Tom arranged for an immediate test inspection of the second headless giant robot. The final assembly of its metal body was taking place and Tom watched as the huge jointed skeleton was set up. Motors were being fastened in place to rigid tubular braces.

To offset the heat generated by the mechanisms inside the robot body, Tom had devised a circulatory cooling system which was now being installed.

Arvid Hanson, standing near Tom, asked, "How does the cooler work?"

Tom explained that it was a highly paramagnetic fluid which was alternately magnetized and demagnetized at a rate controlled by a thermostat.

"It keeps the robot's inside temperature at 96.4 degrees," Tom added.

"I see," Hanson said. "But what about protection from outside heat—the kind your robot will have to withstand in the atomic energy plant?"

"Oh, I'm using asbestalon," Tom replied. This was a material composed of asbestos fibers in a plastic matrix.

Hanson was shaking his head. "When I make a model of this robot for your office," he said, wincing, "it'll be some job to get that chain mail you're using over the moving joints down to scale."

Late that afternoon Tom ran tests on both giant robots and was highly pleased with the results. All the motors were working perfectly. Now only the television-camera eyes in the heads remained to be completed.

"We'll be ready in plenty of time for the first test," he thought, gratified, and walked to his office.

The evening shift was arriving and he greeted Marco who, he knew, would wait patiently to clean the office until he had gone.

Scooping up some unopened letters, Tom slipped them into his pocket and prepared to leave. A final visual check showed everything in place. Files holding secret data were locked. Passing his desk, the young inventor patted the model of his *Sky Queen* and left the office.

"Good night," he said to the watchman, who was standing in the hall.

"Have a pleasant evening," Marco replied.

Tom headed for the building exit. He was the last one out. Reaching the outer plant gate, the young inventor suddenly remembered that he had forgotten to bring a sketch of the robot's face which he planned to work on that evening at home. Turning back, Tom let himself into the locked office building and started down the hall.

Suddenly he saw something that made him freeze in his tracks. Marco was tiptoeing out of the Swifts' private office, his left arm wrapped tightly around the silver model of Tom's *Sky Queen!*

CHAPTER 12

THE SECRET RECORDER

"MARCO!" Tom shouted. "Stop!"

It was a strict rule that nothing was to be removed from the Swifts' private office and Tom was at a loss to know why it had been disobeyed.

"Where are you taking that model?" Tom demanded.

The watchman gave a start, nearly dropping the replica of the Flying Lab.

"Why—er—you're back," he stammered.

"What are you doing with the model, I asked," Tom persisted.

"Why—uh—I've always admired it, Tom." The man hesitated. "That's why I have it now."

Tom was blunt. "What do you mean?"

"I was going to give it a thorough cleaning."

"A cleaning!" Tom was genuinely puzzled. Was Marco sincere? As far as the young inventor knew, the watchman was trustworthy. "You always dust it in the office, don't you?"

"Why, yes. But this time I wanted to get it extra clean. I—I wanted to make the surface clear before varnishing the wings."

"I see," Tom replied. "Don't bother to do it now, Marco. Please put the model back on my desk."

"All right," Marco agreed, and turned and walked slowly back to the office, cradling the silver wings in his arms.

"I do believe I frightened the poor man," Tom thought, as he looked for the drawing which he had come back to get. "Still, it's strange that he would deliberately break a rule." Tom stared at the model. "And it doesn't need varnishing. Now why—"

Tom sat in the office for a long while, thinking. He drummed his fingers on the desk, turning over the events of the day in his mind. He kept coming back to the scene with Marco. The watchman's explanation was far from reassuring, but Tom hated to think that Marco had meant any harm.

On a hunch Tom dropped in at the security office. If there was anything sinister behind Marco's strange behavior, perhaps it might show up in his records.

The files had been reduced to microcards. Tom dialed Marco's individual history key number. The scanner machine quickly located the correct card.

Marco's card held sixty pages of facts on a three-by-five-inch surface. Tom slipped the card into the projector and skimmed through the man's record.

"Not a thing against him," Tom told himself.

Marco had not held many jobs and all of them had been positions of trust. Previous to becoming a night watchman for the Swift offices at the Enterprises plant six months ago, he had been a special guard at a private mental hospital in the Midwest named Blackstone. Several references from former employers praised him highly.

Tom snapped off the projector. "I've been too jumpy lately," he muttered, and decided to go home.

After working a short while on the sketch of the robot's head, Tom retired, but hours later he was still awake. Try as he might, he could not rid himself of a deep mistrust that was consuming him. Enterprises harbored a treacherous enemy. Who was it?

The young inventor knew he could not rest until he had found the answer. Something about Marco's attitude disturbed him. Unable to sleep, Tom decided to go back to work at the plant. He arose, dressed quietly so as not to waken his family, and drove to Swift Enterprises.

Quietly he let himself into the office building. The hallway was deserted. Walking quickly he came to his private office and found the door open. He slipped in.

The light was on, but no one was inside. Tom's eyes roved to the desk. The model of the Flying Lab was gone!

Tom was furious. Whom did Marco think he was fooling? What sort of mysterious game was he play-

ing with the model of the Flying Lab as a pawn?
Before his anger had time to subside, he heard footsteps in the hall. Instinctively Tom hid behind a
large overstuffed chair.

Marco entered the office, carrying the model. He
carefully set it on the desk in exactly the same position Tom had left it. Then he turned and hurried
out of the room.

"Well, for Pete's sake!" Tom muttered to himself.

For an instant he was set to leap up from behind
the chair and go after the man. But he was puzzled.
He had to find out what made his ornamental desk
piece so important.

Gingerly Tom lifted the craft and examined it
closely. At first glance there was nothing to indicate

Marco carefully set the model on the desk in

that the model had been tampered with, yet something seemed different. Tom studied it at various angles.

"I know!" he murmured. "The plane's heavier than it was—weighs several ounces more than it did!"

Tom began to manipulate each of the moving parts. He spun the wheels, then turned his attention to the control surfaces. He flipped the model's rudder. Suddenly the bottom fell out, along with a reel of recording tape.

Dumfounded, Tom snatched up the tiny reel,

exactly the same position Tom had left it

then peered into the model. Within he saw a spindle and a recording head. Reaching in, he pulled out part of a miniature tape recorder.

"Very clever," he muttered. "An ingenious machine with a built-in amplifier, its own power supply, and a tiny microphone strong enough to pull in a roomful of conversation."

Tom noticed that the degree of miniaturization involved bore a striking resemblance to that used in the mechanical crow.

"The same enemy!" he thought. "But one thing's sure. It can't be Marco. He's a stooge for some brain."

But here at last was the source of the leak! This was how news was getting out! Tom and his associates had been broadcasting their most secret plans during their frequent office conferences. Each night Marco probably would change the tape.

The young inventor was sorely tempted to reach in and rip the wiring to shreds. Instead, he sat down and thought over the full implication of the espionage attempt. Then, cautiously, he rewound the tape and set it back in operation.

"Marco must not know I've found out. Before I leave for the Citadel this afternoon, I'll dictate a misleading series of statements about the trip to the West and about the relotrol." Sighing, he continued to speculate, "Since the most recent tape is probably on its way to the enemy, it's a good thing there weren't any secret projects discussed here in the office today."

Right now, Tom decided, it was important that Marco's every move be watched. He slipped from the building without being seen and drove home rapidly. He went at once to the attic where he kept a short-wave radio, used for top-secret communication. Another was set up at Radnor's home.

It was four in the morning when the security officer's sound sleep was shattered by the squeals of the set's speaker. Groggy, he felt for the microphone.

"Wh-what is it?" he mumbled.

"It's Tom. Rad, I've traced the security leak!"

"What!" Radnor was wide awake in an instant. Tom explained what he had learned.

"Great going!" Radnor exclaimed. "Marco leaves the plant in another three hours. I'll have him followed. Security will put one of our night men on the job right away."

When Tom hung up, his troubled mind was relieved. At last the mystery was taking shape. He fell into bed and drifted off into the first peaceful sleep he had had in days.

While Tom slept, Radnor's men began to draw the net around the unsuspecting watchman. A series of check points were set up along the route to Marco's home. His house was placed under immediate surveillance. Less than an hour after Tom's conversation with Radnor, a plant detective was posted in the corridor to watch Marco's every move.

When morning came the watchman punched out and left for home. The detective followed as Marco took the expected route, deviating only once, to drop a fat letter in a mailbox.

When Tom arrived at the plant, he went straight to the security office. Radnor was there, studying Marco's personnel record.

"I'm going to double check this information, Tom," he said. "We'll investigate his background again. I'll sift through every one of Marco's acquaintances, in the hope of linking him with the Briggin gang."

"Where do you think you'll start?" Tom asked, thumbing through the reports.

"My first stop is Blackstone," said Radnor, consulting his casebook. "I'll talk to everyone who ever knew Marco at that mental institution. Where can I reach you?"

"I plan to leave this afternoon for the Citadel. Everything's ready and I may as well go."

"Then I'll be in touch with you at the atomic energy plant."

Suddenly Tom remembered that he must dictate misinformation into the recorder hidden in the *Sky Queen* model before he left. When he finished he smiled to himself. The false facts should throw the enemy off, at least for a while.

Phyl and Sandy were on hand early that afternoon, packed and ready for the trip. The repaired *Sky*

Queen, fresh from the plane shops and completely overhauled, was raised from her hangar.

The fuselage gleamed in the sunlight as the great ship was rolled onto a loading apron. The girls went aboard immediately. Then Tom, Bud, Arvid Hanson, and chief patternmaking engineer Hank Sterling, who was going along on the trip, supervised the loading of the cargo.

The first item of importance was Stan Lee, a flat-faced walking robot with which Tom was planning to make experiments in entering and leaving the atomic plant. Next came a drone plane, to be set in motion above the Citadel. Last to be rolled aboard was the squat, angular-looking helicopter, the *Skeeter.*

When all was in readiness, the girls asked where Chow was.

"At your service," the cook replied, running up in the loudest shirt the onlookers had ever seen.

"Wow!" Bud cried. "You trying to set the plane on fire again?"

Chow grinned and looked down at his bright-red luminous shirt. "Why, brand my Texas general store, I think this here is right purty! But don't you make fun o' my southwest buyin'. Look what I picked up right in Shopton."

From his bag he pulled out a brilliant gold-and-green plaid shirt. "That's what held me up."

"It would stop anything!" Bud needled.

The travelers waved good-by to their families and

friends and went aboard. The *Sky Queen* blasted its exhaust fire at the ground. The silver body quivered and ascended in a direct line until it was ten thousand feet over Shopton. Then Tom cut in the forward power and headed for the West.

CHAPTER 13

ARV UNDER SUSPICION

FAR ABOVE the commercial air lanes, Tom set the *Sky Queen* on automatic pilot, making sure the radarscope and its warning bell were operating, and headed for the atomic energy plant. Cloud formations obscured the earth below, and the passengers, comfortably settled in the lounge, began to talk.

"Tom," said Phyl Newton, "please bring me up to date on exactly what your giant robot is going to do—and what experiment Stan Lee will carry on."

The young inventor smiled. He was sure that Sandy, who had a good knowledge of the whole setup, had told her friend a great deal about it. He endeavored to think up phases of the project which Phyl might not have heard.

"As you know, after the atomic pile starts work in its separate concrete shelter," Tom began, "nothing living could survive in there. Even if the pile's activities were stopped, and it were emptied of uranium, the radioactivity would kill a man.

"So, until now, repairs on the plant haven't been possible, in case something should go wrong in it."

Phyl interrupted to ask what breakdowns could occur inside the plant. Tom said there were many potential difficulties. Leaks might develop in the cooling system which would lead to corrosion. The cadmium rods might wear out, or break, or even become jammed in their sleeves.

"Thermocouples—electric thermometers used to measure the temperature—may require replacement," Tom went on. "Then, as you know, any building is affected by weather and ground disturbances. The concrete in the inner plant may crack and have to be repaired with mortar. Certain iron parts will rust and these must be painted from time to time—two more very necessary jobs for the giant robot."

Bud remarked that there was one important use for the robot that Tom had not mentioned. "It has to do with sabotage," he said.

"How in the world could there be sabotage when the Citadel is so well protected?" Phyl asked.

"Easy," said Sandy. "Somebody could drop a bomb on the plant."

"That's why I'm going to set up a system of drone planes over Dad's plant," said Tom. "Then, too, anyone who got past our security officers might manufacture a bomb that looked like one of the uranium slugs and send it in with the regular slugs."

Bud whistled. "When that exploded, good night! No more atomic energy plant."

"But that won't be the case at the Citadel," Tom said. "Even a bomb detonating inside it would not ruin the whole plant. But only the robot could restore the damaged pile to working order."

"Tell me more about Stan Lee's job," Phyl said.

"All he's going to do this trip," said Tom, "is walk around. First, I want to be sure that the control board is working properly. Second, that Stan Lee makes the turns at the right time, and responds inside the building when he gets the signal."

There was a knock at the rear of the lounge and the young people turned to see Chow standing there with a wide grin on his face. He was holding a large tray heaped with sandwiches, cookies, and milk.

"If you-all kin stop conferrin' long enough for a lil ole Texas snack, I'll be glad to bring this forward."

"Bring 'em along!" Bud cried. "What's in those sandwiches, though? Hope they're not cactus specials. I'm not *that* starved!"

Chow ignored Bud's remarks as he set the tray on a permanent wall table.

"I always said," he drawled, "if you use your haid too hard you forgit your stomach and then you gits into trouble. Yup—a lil ole snack now an' then keeps you agoin'."

Sandy laughed and said she could not think of any

nicer way to keep going. But Bud was not inclined
to let the chef off so easily. He bit into one of the
sandwiches, choked, and cried:

"Man! This is worse than cactus! Tastes like cement and red peppers!"

The former chuck-wagon cook looked hurt. "Bud
Barclay, you-all don't know a good thing when you
eat it. That's jest a plain old chicken sandwich—
with some ground-up nuts and horseradish sauce.
I learned about it from a Chinese cook."

"Well, you can give that recipe back to your
Chinese friend," retorted Bud. There actually were
tears in his eyes and Chow finally admitted that perhaps he had put too much horseradish in the sandwich.

Suddenly Bud realized that he had not chosen the
sandwich himself. Chow had handed it to him. He
looked at the cook with suspicion in his eyes. But
before he could say anything more, Chow fled.

Tom roared with laughter. "I guess after this,
Bud, you'll think twice before you kid Chow about
his cooking."

The rest of the food was delicious, and Sterling
and Hanson declared that if it were a sample of the
meals they were to have on the rest of the trip, they
would vote Chow the best cook in the West.

Two hours later they were winging over eroded
scrub country and Tom went back to the pilot's seat.
Below the ship great black boulders, cracked by
weathering, were strewn about like so many pebbles.

Rusty valleys of clay, splotched with green rivulets and caked yellow terraces, broke the plains into forked patterns.

There was not a sign of civilization. Here and there yucca trees poked their spines into the arid air. A few minutes later they were flying over a vast level area, obviously smoothed by man's efforts.

"Here we are!" Tom announced.

On the flat surface stood a cluster of ultramodern structures. Standing apart at one edge were dormitories. Laboratory and office buildings were scattered in a loose pinwheel formation around the perimeter.

From its center rose a long, massive boxlike rectangle. The concrete building was windowless, its thick walls broken only by ventilating shafts. This was the building to house the atomic pile. It would be encased in concrete, deep within the building's double walls.

As Tom circled once over the area, Bud asked where they would land.

"About ten miles from here," Tom replied, flying away from the plant, "halfway between the nearest town and the Citadel. More convenient for all of us that way."

Presently he cut the forward engines and set the jet lifters in motion. Then, gradually, he cut power and the ship touched ground. As the travelers got out, Phyl remarked:

"Look at all this space! Just rocks and desert as far as you can see!"

Tom cautioned the girls about wearing their boots at all times while walking around. "Watch out for snakes and poisonous Gila monsters," he warned.

It had been arranged that Bud and the girls would live in the *Sky Queen,* with Chow as chaperon. They would carry on their sightseeing from there by helicopter. Tom would commute back and forth to the Citadel by jeep.

"If that cloud of dust out there is what I think it is," he said, "a fleet of our trucks is coming to meet us now and carry the equipment back."

A few minutes later the trucks rolled up to the plane, kicking dust and sand in every direction. Three of the vehicles were to take Tom, Sterling, Hanson, and equipment to the plant. The fourth was on its way to the only nearby settlement to pick up mail.

"While I'm getting the robot set up," Tom said to Bud, "why don't you act as the girls' escort. You might enjoy a visit to town right now on the mail truck. I've heard that it's an old, one-street, frontier-type setup with all the pioneer-day atmosphere."

Intrigued at the thought, the girls and Bud climbed aboard the truck, and rode off.

Tom, Sterling, and Hanson, using cranes and hoists from the Flying Lab, loaded the small walking robot onto one truck and derricked the drone plane onto the trailer of another.

At six o'clock the convoy set out to navigate the wasteland stretch to the plant. The vehicles picked their way over the terrain, avoiding boulders and gullies.

As they rode along, Tom and his two technical advisers, who were alone in one truck, discussed their plans. Tom voiced the hope that the misinformation he had dictated on the tape recorder in his office would reach the Briggin gang and prevent another encounter with them.

"Don't count on that wish too much, Tom," warned Hank Sterling, who had been staring up at the sky. "Look at the formation of crows coming over the horizon."

The flock of large birds, black against the sun, were winging their way directly toward the course being followed by the trucks. Tom watched tensely. In a matter of seconds the two paths would intersect as the trucks moved out of the shadow of a nearby mesa!

"Get ready to break up the motorcade line," Tom radioed to the other trucks. Then to Hanson he said, "Take a look at them through your binoculars."

Hanson grabbed the binoculars and trained them on the birds. "They're not crows!" he reported. "Real or mechanical. They're vultures!"

They all breathed easier and Tom reversed his order to the drivers ahead of him.

"I never thought I'd be so happy to see vultures," he said with a wry smile. "I still have hopes that they'll believe the false facts I dictated and start looking for us down in Louisiana."

"Are you sure they got that message?" Hank asked.

"We can only hope Marco mails that one too," Tom said. "By the way, Rad is out at Blackstone Hospital checking on all patients and workers with whom Marco might have been friendly."

Hank gave a start. "You think some mental case might be mixed up in this deal?"

"Could be," said Tom.

As the line of vehicles drew closer to the Citadel, Tom and the others became aware of its immense size. Though they were still a mile away, the buildings loomed up like a vast fortress.

At last they reached the outer barbed-wire electrified fence surrounding the entire installation. Tom stopped before a wide gate where a guard's shack stood. The other trucks rolled to a stop, one behind another.

A uniformed member of the security police approached Tom's truck. "This the Swift party?" he inquired, glancing in the cab.

"That's right," replied Tom, pleased to note that security measures were being enforced. "Here are our passes. I'm Tom Swift. This is Mr. Sterling and Mr. Hanson."

The uniformed guard took the passes, examined them, and said Tom and Hank might enter. Then he shook his head. "I'm sorry, but we can't admit you, Mr. Hanson."

"What!" Tom almost jumped out of the cab.

"This man is our chief modelmaker. He built the scale replica of this plant!"

Hanson was speechless. Hank Sterling leaned over, angry and puzzled. "Why can't he be admitted?"

"His security clearance papers haven't come through from the FBI," replied the guard. "I don't care who he is. He doesn't get through this post. We received clearance for you and Tom Swift Jr., but not for Hanson."

Tom swung open the door and leaped to the ground. He realized that the sentry was doing his job as directed and would not give in.

"Give me your sentry phone," Tom requested in a firm but polite tone.

He called the plant office and spoke to his father. In a short time Mr. Swift arrived at the gate.

"I know nothing about any of this, Tom!" declared the elder inventor. "I can't understand it! We requested clearance for all three of you."

Tom could no longer restrain his impatience. He jiggled the telephone hook. "Get me long-distance," he told the operator, beckoning to the security guard to listen in on the call.

He explained the urgency of the call and received an immediate line to Washington. A check with the Federal Bureau of Investigation revealed that all three sets of clearance papers had been sent by them. Dashing back to Hanson, he said:

"You're in the clear, Arv. Washington is telegraphing confirmation immediately." The young inventor looked grim. "But it doesn't explain what happened to your papers. I wonder if our enemies could somehow have gotten hold of them just to delay us?"

The guard apologized to Hanson and the gate was raised to allow the motorcade to enter.

Later, on the inspection trip through the various laboratories and workshops, Tom and Sterling and Hanson found themselves nodding in approval of the ingenious design and fine engineering of the layout. At last Mr. Swift led them to the main structure, built of white cement. Inside was a corridor extending around four inner walls of lead and concrete. On one of the walls was a relay and television board for messages to and from the robot as he worked in the inner room. The main remote-control panel was in a separate building.

"Tom, I expect your giant to be able to feed slugs of uranium to the oven if necessary," Mr. Swift said.

"He'll do it," Tom assured his father.

"Now we'll take a look at the heart of this building," Mr. Swift said.

In the huge interior section was a mass of square lead and concrete pipes arranged longitudinally.

"Looks like a mammoth honeycomb," Hank remarked. "I suppose the slugs of uranium are fed to the pile through these."

"Correct," said Mr. Swift. "The heart of the reactor is in the center. In there the uranium will be bombarded with neutrons and changed into the various transuranium elements. Then the slugs are taken from the pile and the robot separates out the new elements in his own completely equipped chemistry lab over there." He pointed to an enclosure whose walls were lined with the necessary chemicals in radiation-proof containers. "After that, he prepares them for shipment to medical and scientific institutions."

"And where will the waste products—such as the slug casings—go?" Hanson asked.

"Tom's robot will carry them out through a tunnel to an underground lake we've made. In that way, no living thing can be contaminated by the radioactive waste."

Next, Mr. Swift took them outdoors to a small concrete structure located at a short distance from the pile plant.

"This is where Tom and the other operators will receive reports from the robot and send him orders," Mr. Swift explained.

From the outside the structure resembled a gun pillbox more than a control house. Within, however, the function of the building was obvious, with its large color-television screen, surrounded by loudspeakers and banks of oscillographs. Control knobs and buttons were set into a huge desk-height panel. Hank Sterling and Arv Hanson examined the large racks of amplifiers with interest.

Tom now showed them the tape library. "These

tapes will be a real boon to the robot's operator," he said. "They'll do away with the necessity of direct control on routine acts and motions of the robot. In fact, we can feed in any of more than a thousand different tapes with directions to get him out of every difficulty we've been able to foresee. But when something unexpected comes up, the operator will have to take over."

"It's amazing," Hanson commented. "I'm beginning to have a lot of respect for that giant robot as well as his inventor."

"Thanks." Tom laughed. "Well, I guess we've seen all we can today. Tomorrow I start work with Stan Lee."

He, Arv, and Hank spent the night in one of the dormitories and were up early the next morning to start work. After breakfast, the elder inventor said:

"I guess, son, you're eager to see the tunnel through which the robot will descend and enter the plant. You'll find it built to your specifications."

"Good," said Tom, grinning. He had been worried about clearance, since his giant robot's antenna would need every last fraction of an inch to get through.

Mr. Swift reminded his son that the tunnel had just been completed. "So watch your step, Tom. There may be some loose debris and chunks of concrete that haven't been cleared out."

"I will, Dad."

The others walked with him to the opening and

A blinding flash enveloped the opening above him

peered down into the tunnel. There was a metal rung ladder to the bottom which would later be replaced by a ramp for the giant robot's convenience.

Holding his flashlight, Tom started lowering himself, clinging to the ladder. As he grasped the third rung, a blinding flash suddenly enveloped the opening above him.

The ladder snapped apart and the young inventor toppled to the tunnel floor!

CHAPTER 14

STRANGE INDIAN STORY

LOOSE EARTH and cement showered down upon Tom. Sputtering and choking, he fought his way through the mound of debris and gasped for breath in the dust-filled cavern.

Above him there was a deathlike silence and he was worried about the safety of his father and friends. Tom knew that the only way to get aboveground was through the tunnel and into the plant.

His flashlight was buried in the debris and he stumbled along the black passageway, feeling his way inch by inch to avoid any pitfalls.

A hundred thoughts filled his mind at once. What had caused the blast? All detonating had been completed months earlier when foundations for the plant were being dug. Surely no workman could have been carrying dynamite at this late date. But then, what?

A dim light ahead indicated that he was approaching the basement floor of the building that housed the pile. He broke into a run and presently found himself in the vast underground room. It was well lighted. At its center concrete pillars, twelve feet square and looking even larger because of the low ceiling, supported the framework of the pile on the floor above.

Tom looked around for an exit, found a door, and hastened upstairs. He was between the double walls in the section known as the "hot" corridor because of its nearness to the pile. He started running again, first to the left and then, remembering that the exit was in the other direction, to the right. At last he came to the familiar sight of the relay board and the exit.

Outside, the scene that greeted his eyes was one of disorder. Planks and bricks from piles of construction material had been scattered all over. Nurses and doctors were administering to the injured. Two ambulances were parked near the tunnel entrance. Tom hurried toward the scene of confusion.

"Dad!" he cried. Mr. Swift was seated on an ambulance cot, holding a gauze compress to his head. He called excitedly to his son:

"Tom, Tom! Are you all right?"

"I'm fine, Dad. What happened? Where are Hank and Arv?"

"Hanson got a bump on his head from a flying stone. Sterling's gone to the plant hospital to have a leg cut treated."

"Anybody badly hurt?" Tom asked.

"Fortunately no. And not a soul saw what caused the blast."

At this moment a security guard came racing up. In his hands were several metal fragments.

"We found these in the blast area, Mr. Swift," he panted. "They're sections of casing from a large bomb."

"Have these pieces been analyzed?" Mr. Swift asked.

"The labs are going over some of the fragments now," the guard replied. "We think the bomb must have been dropped by a plane that was out of the range of our radarscope."

Tom and his father exchanged glances. "The Briggin boys?" they were asking themselves.

"Or some crank who is opposed to atomic progress and wants us all back in the Stone Age," Tom thought ruefully. Aloud he said, "Dad, this plant needs drone protection badly. I'm sorry we were able to bring only one with us. But I'll drop everything else and get it in the air as soon as possible. Meanwhile, we can order more from Shopton."

A half hour later Hank and Arv insisted that they felt all right and wanted to help Tom with the task. They followed him to the trailer on which the drone plane rested.

The sleek robot craft was rolled off an incline and along the ground. The three of them pushed it to a wide expanse of clearing.

A curious crowd of atomic scientists and workmen gathered around to observe as Tom rigged up a portable patrolscope and beeper box for the drone. The plant's electricians helped him run a Citadel power line to the controls. First came a ground test with Tom working the controls. The ailerons flapped, the rudder turned, and the elevators moved and pivoted, all in response to his directions.

"Now for the test flight," Tom said, after exhaustive checks had been completed. "Conditions here are a lot different from those at Fearing Island. A low-flying drone might not respond fast enough to avoid hitting a sharp rock formation or a mesa."

"We'll have to test it for any possible static interference that it might encounter from the operation of the plant," his father commented.

Now the grueling air tests began. While Tom manipulated the beeper controls, the drone swept across the blue expanse of western sky. A silver streak, it darted in and out of jagged rock formations, and sliced through deep crevasses. Suddenly the robot plane heeled over, out of control.

"What is it, Tom?" asked Hank.

"These rock mesas—they reflect signals as in a television 'ghost' picture."

Tom knew the drone must climb fast, as if on an interception mission. Reaching the pinnacle of the climb, the drone regained its equilibrium.

"Whew!" Arv exclaimed in relief.

A few moments later Tom landed the ship.

"I'll have to arrange a series of compensating directional towers for the signal," said Tom. "We can probably have the drone in the air by tomorrow. It will be set in a pattern to fly continuously over the plant."

Tom decided to wire the Enterprises plant for additional drones to be ferried to the Citadel.

"We'll need five more drones and a permanent control board," he said, "before I'll be satisfied that the protection here is adequate."

By the time Tom had worked out the specifications for the drone-control towers and turned them over to the engineers, it was dinnertime. He told his father that he planned to spend the night at the Flying Lab. He drove over in a jeep and was amazed to see a horse tethered near the *Sky Queen*. He parked and hurried up the ladder to the giant plant.

Reaching the doorway he stared in astonishment. Standing before him, arms folded, stood a tall, well-built Indian wearing buckskins and a denim shirt.

"Tom," called Sandy over the man's shoulder, "we were just going to drive over to the plant to find you. This is Chief Rob Featherlight of the local Zuñi tribe. We visited his reservation today."

Tom relaxed and smiled. His sister had wasted no time in becoming acquainted with her neighbors. And apparently this neighbor was just as curious about their activities.

"This is a very fine plane," the young Indian remarked, as the group seated themselves in the lounge.

"The chief told us something this afternoon which I think you should hear from him at once, Tom," Sandy said.

The chief began his story. "There is trouble on my reservation. It has been caused by a large black crow. The bird has been flying overhead every day, just before sunset."

Tom exchanged glances with the others.

"But this crow," Featherlight went on, "does not fly like a crow. It banks like a plane does, not like a bird. Sometimes it flies at a speed so great as to bring fear to the hearts of my people. The older members of the council believe the bird to be an evil spirit that has returned to earth in this unnatural form." The chief paused a moment, then added, "I have been educated at public schools and know better."

"This crow," Tom asked excitedly, "did it ever come near the ground?"

"Only once. A young brave, our finest bow-and-arrow champion, tried to shoot it down. But the arrows just bounced off."

Tom's brow creased with worry. There was no doubt in his mind that the bird was one of the sinister mechanical crows that had tried to kill him!

Sandy looked at her brother with eyes filled with fear. "Oh, Tom, I'm scared. You're not safe anywhere!"

CHAPTER 15

A CRUCIAL TEST

CHIEF FEATHERLIGHT stared perplexed at the Swifts and their friends. Tom told him that the bird was mechanical and remote controlled, probably from a plane. Leaving all the gruesome details out of the story, he concluded by saying:

"The crow is the work of a scientist who is trying to get his hands on some of our secret inventions. I'm sure that he intends no harm to the Zuñis. Tell your people not to worry. The crow was only on a test flight."

The Indian seemed satisfied and arose, saying he would follow Tom's advice. The young inventor asked the chief to keep him informed of any further appearances of the crow. The man nodded, then descended the ladder and rode off on his horse.

Chow relaxed the tension somewhat by ringing a big dinner bell he had brought along on the trip. It never failed to get a smile.

The cook announced that a barbecue would be served under the stars. Everyone scrambled for the door.

Chow had arranged dinner chuck-wagon style. The girls perched on rocks and the boys sat cross-legged, Indian-fashion, around a crackling fire of charcoal.

As Chow broiled huge slabs of meat, Mr. Swift came to join them and spend the night.

"Yes, sir," said the talented chef, winking slyly at Tom, "there's nothin' like an open fire for steak. That's the way lizard meat was meant to be enjoyed."

Sandy refused to smile. She could not forget the danger that hung over her brother's every move.

"You've got to do something, Tom," she said finally.

"I'm taking reasonable precautions," her brother replied lightly. Then, as a joke, he added, "Do you want me to walk around with a distorter in my hat?"

"Yes," said Sandy. "That would be a very good idea."

"I agree," Phyl added. "That's just what you need. We'd worry a lot less."

Bud remarked that the girls were right. "Practically speaking," he said, "it would just be a matter of making a distorter small enough to fit into a hat." He envisioned a miniature apparatus resting on the inner crown frame of a ten-gallon hat.

Tom had already pulled a pencil from his pocket

and was drawing a diagram on the ground. "It could be done," he said. "The antenna would still work on a scale of, say—" He paused. "But I don't have a hat big enough."

The tension had been broken and the evening was spent pleasantly with Chow spinning yarns of the old West for Bud and the girls while Tom worked late in the plane's laboratory, redesigning the distorter to small scale.

The next morning a stack of flapjacks was waiting on the lounge table when the four young people and Mr. Swift appeared. Beside them lay three ten-gallon hats.

"Where did these come from?" Tom asked, puzzled.

Chow grinned. "I picked 'em up from the general store in town."

"Charles Winkler!" Tom exclaimed. "You old rascal! Why, you didn't know until last night that I wanted one."

Tom knew that Chow, a loyal horseman, never drove a jeep. And pintos were not part of the *Sky Queen's* equipment.

"How'd you get to town?" Tom asked.

"Why, brand the sunrise," said the cook, "an early-morning walk does wonders for the appetite!"

"I know how you cowboys love to hike!" scoffed Tom, remembering it was a ten-mile walk to town. "Come on, Chow, give. Where did you get them?"

Chow said, with a twinkle in his eyes, that the ten-gallon hats were for Tom, Mr. Swift, and Bud. "You kin put them there dees-torters in as many as you like." But he steadfastly refused to divulge his secret.

They all thanked him and Tom added, "I built two midget distorters during the night. Dad, I'll install one in your hat and the other in mine. I guess Bud won't need one to hunt for Indian treasure."

Bud had promised the girls that he would help them explore Purple Mesa. After breakfast the boys rolled the *Skeeter* out of the hangar. Tom helped his sister and Phyl aboard while Bud checked the fuel supply of the squat helicopter. Through the *Skeeter's* wide windows, Tom could see Sandy loading her camera. Phyl, her sketching pad under her arm, waved happily in anticipation of the day's fun.

Bud climbed into the pilot's seat. Four jet-tipped rotor blades began to rotate slowly at first, then whirled at tremendous speed. The ship rose slowly through the cloud of sand it had stirred up on the desert floor.

The bright-red helicopter made a gay picture as it sailed off with the sightseers. Tom watched until the craft was out of sight. Then he turned to the more serious matter of robot testing at the plant.

A crew had been at work since sunup with cranes and power shovels, clearing out the debris in the tunnel. When Tom and his father arrived they were able to put Stan Lee into action immediately. The flat-faced, man-sized robot created even more of a stir among the scientists than the drone plane had.

Tom instructed the guards to keep everyone well back from the tunnel, however, in case of more trouble. He hoped that the circling drone plane would keep any unfriendly craft from the area.

Tom planned to walk the test robot through the tunnel and into the plant where it would simulate the route to be taken by the giant robot. He would use only the portable control board he had brought along.

The robot was lowered to the floor of the tunnel. For the complex journey, Tom had inserted three simultaneous action tapes in the control panel. As Mr. Swift beamed a powerful torch into the gaping hole, Tom closed the switch that started the tapes. There was a faint whir as metal prongs scanned the tapes for instruction holes.

In a moment Stan Lee began to advance stiffly into the tunnel. Then he was out of sight. His movements now would be known only by the blinker lights on the control board.

"He'll make several turns following the tunnel," Tom remarked. "When he reaches the pile room, he should do a complete about-face and be back here in twenty minutes."

But five minutes later the lights for the first turn blinked a steady danger sign. Stan Lee was in trouble!

Tom shut off the power. "He may have fallen, Dad!"

Quickly descending the ladder, Tom ran through

the tunnel. The robot had lost his balance on what should have been a relatively easy turn. He had landed face down and dented his chest.

Tom was shaking his head in puzzlement when his father joined him at the end of the tunnel. "This turn should have been almost automatic. Stan Lee performed it flawlessly many times in Shopton."

"It's very strange," Mr. Swift agreed.

The two studied the situation, rechecking the relays. Tom proposed that the answer might be right above their heads in the distorter hats.

"I hardly think so," Mr. Swift answered. "Those distorters are so small, their field is probably much too weak to interfere. There may be some factor in the plant that we've overlooked."

The Swifts returned to the Citadel's office to check blueprints and electrical-installation maps. The plant engineers delved deep into their files and unrolled large sheets of building plans showing where power-cable ducts lay. None of these, however, were near enough to the tunnel to interfere with the operation of the robot.

"I'm convinced that it's something more deep-seated than this," said Tom, after the scientists had left the room. "Stan Lee went out of control in the same way our jet plane did when it was captured by the crow, Dad."

"But our radarmen haven't reported anything flying near the Citadel," Mr. Swift said.

Tom nodded, frowning. "There's no getting

around it, Dad. Someone took over the robot controls from inside the plant. But how?"

Suddenly the young inventor cried, "Dad, the missing relotrol! Maybe it's been brought here."

"Impossible, Tom. The only people who enter the plant are known—" He stopped and stared at his son. "You mean we'd better look at the plant's personnel records?"

"Exactly, Dad."

Mr. Swift led his son to the security file in the main office.

"I don't know what we'll find here," the elder inventor said. "Every man is a top scientist. Three of them, the greatest in their respective fields. This card, for instance"—he held up a file microcard—"contains the record of one of the greatest physicists of our day, Robert Turnbull.

"The man has a number of research inventions to his credit, including the famous Turnbull Mesonator. His entire family is scientifically gifted. He has an identical twin brother named Raymond, who is also an atomic physicist. He was a brilliant man but is now mentally ill."

"What happened, Dad?"

"The old story of a sensitive mind, overworked, I assume. My guess is that Raymond broke down from sheer mental exhaustion during his intensive research work."

Tom expressed sympathy and asked when the breakdown had occurred.

"Oh, about a year ago. Just before his brother Robert joined us here at the Citadel."

At that moment the blinker on the short-wave radio set lighted up. A message from Shopton was coming through.

"This is Phil Radnor!" barked the speaker. "We have a further report on Marco's activities while he was employed at Blackstone Mental Hospital. He seems to have been very friendly with one of the patients—a Raymond Turnbull—who has escaped!"

CHAPTER 16

THE VULTURES RETURN

AS RADNOR PAUSED after his startling announcement that the mentally ill scientist was missing, Tom exclaimed:

"Rad, I want all the facts on the Turnbull escape! Get me the exact date."

Radnor reported that the escape had taken place exactly one month before.

"And what a month it's been!" Tom thought, remembering the attacks by crows on his jet plane and later the *Sky Queen*.

The loss of the relotrol had been followed by desperate attempts on the part of the Briggin gang to secure a robot. First the phony magician. Then the disguised Zoltan. Later Marco's strange behavior. A bomb at the plant and now a crow nearby.

"There must be some connection," Tom decided.

After he finished his talk with Radnor, he turned to his father and expressed his suspicions.

"It seems incredible that a man of Raymond Turnbull's reputation would stoop to associating with bank robbers," Mr. Swift said. "But a sick mind can lead to odd actions."

"Dad, how sure are you of Robert Turnbull's loyalty? Could he be mixed up in this thing too?"

Mr. Swift replied thoughtfully, "I can't believe he is guilty of any disloyalty to me. But I wonder how much he may know about his twin's recent activities."

"Don't you think that we should talk with Robert Turnbull at once?" Tom urged.

"Yes, son. I certainly don't want to cast suspicion on someone who may be innocent. But we must get to the bottom of this plot before our work and scientific progress is brought to a complete standstill."

They went immediately to the scientist's lab. Robert Turnbull was an erect, handsome man of fifty. With dark eyes set deep in his pale face, he looked quizzically at his visitors but greeted them affably. The Swifts told him of the report at once.

Robert Turnbull listened in silence for several minutes, then suddenly he flung his lab apron angrily to the floor.

"Mr. Swift, I'm shocked at your insinuations!" he snapped.

"I believe," said Mr. Swift with dignity, "that if

you were in my place you would make an investigation too."

Turnbull calmed down a bit. Retrieving his apron, he tilted back on the lab stool and regarded Mr. Swift and his son curiously. "I suffered months of abuse and worry because of my twin brother's strange actions before he entered Blackstone. I thought all that was past. Now you come to me with a story of an escape I know nothing about.

"Then you dare to accuse a sick man who has devoted his life to the betterment of humanity of collaborating with criminal elements and conspiring to commit sabotage. No Turnbull would ever be connected with such underhanded treachery!"

"You say you know nothing about your brother's escape?" Tom queried.

"I am shocked by the news and angry that my family has not informed me of it."

"Perhaps they do not know about his escape," Tom ventured.

Robert Turnbull got off the stool so violently that it toppled over. "I must leave at once and contact my family to learn if they have any information about Raymond. Perhaps he has sought shelter with them. Poor Raymond!"

The scientist gathered his work together, scooped up a sheaf of papers, and hurried out of the room. Feeling justified about the questioning but sorry that it had upset Robert Turnbull, the Swifts returned to their own office.

No sooner had they entered than the blinker monitor again registered a call from Shopton.

Tom gave a mock groan and said, "I wonder if this is more trouble?"

From the other end of the line, Radnor's voice was hollow. "Hate to bother you again, but something has come up."

The young inventor steadied himself. "What's wrong, Rad?" he asked tersely.

"Marco is gone!" Rad reported.

Tom winced. Their key contact had vanished!

Radnor said Marco had melted into a downtown crowd, eluding the shadowing detective. The next evening he had not appeared for work. That could only mean the watchman had found out that he was under suspicion.

It also implied that he probably had learned about the fake messages planted on the tape. He might have gathered the real facts through some other source. Tom informed Radnor about the conference with Robert Turnbull, then signed off.

"I'm afraid we're in for more trouble," Tom said, and told his father about Radnor's report.

"The Citadel and everyone in it is probably a target now," Tom continued.

He did not add that he feared for the safety of Sandy and Phyl too. He wished, now, that they had not accompanied him on what was proving to be a hazardous venture.

Meanwhile, the *Skeeter* was riding the canyon updrafts. Under Bud Barclay's skillful handling, the helicopter had covered many miles of scenic eroded rock, hovered directly in front of grotesque pink cliffs, and whirled around jagged, fiery-orange stone formations. He windmilled the craft under a natural limestone arch while Sandy snapped pictures and Phyl drew quick sketches.

Later, they passed over Indian pueblo dwellings. The adobe skyscrapers, heaped atop one another, rose like rock-tiered tables out of the loam. Through binoculars Sandy could plainly see the bright-colored blankets that the Indians used for doors.

After passing over a stretch of rolling land dotted with sagebrush, they saw Purple Mesa. It stood like a solid fortress in the lighter-colored landscape.

"We're almost there!" called Sandy excitedly, as the huge mass loomed before them.

"It's still a number of miles off," Bud observed. "Distances are deceiving out here."

The mesa was indeed several minutes' flying time away. Alone and brooding, it seemed to bear down upon them as they approached.

"Why, it isn't purple at all!" exclaimed Phyl. "It seems to be rust-colored."

"Wait until sunset," Bud remarked.

"We won't be here then," said Phyl, a note of disappointment in her voice. "Tom made us promise to be back by suppertime."

"I'll take the *Skeeter* up. We'll hover over the top and look for a landing place," said Bud.

The helicopter rose alongside the sheer wall of Purple Mesa.

"It *is* steep," gasped Sandy, "and craggy. No wonder nobody's been able to climb it to look for the treasure!"

The cliff's edges had been filed into sharp and fantastic shapes by the countless desert sandstorms. Bud carefully spiraled the *Skeeter* in for a landing on the flat top of the mesa.

"Oh, look!" cried Phyl. "Here comes a family of vultures. They must nest on the mesa."

As Bud held the ship steady, he glanced over his shoulder. The birds were not vultures but metal-feathered jets. They were the death-dealing crows, capable of seizing complete control of the helicopter and dashing it to pieces against the rocks.

Suddenly the ship was buffeted around.

"What's the matter with the *Skeeter?*" Sandy cried.

"The birds!" yelled Bud. He kicked desperately at the control pedals, but it was no use. The stabilizer rotor was out of control and the cabin began to spin.

"Hang on, we're going to crash!" Bud shouted in warning.

The helicopter dropped, hit the edge of the mesa, and plummeted down the side!

CHAPTER 17

MAROONED ON THE MESA

THE *SKEETER* hung on a crag at the edge of the precipice.

"Kick the window!" Bud yelled.

Sandy's foot flew against the large pane of safety glass. The pane popped out and Sandy tumbled out onto the top of the mesa. Phyl scrambled after her just as the helicopter started to roll down the steep cliff.

The girls watched in horror as the craft, with Bud still trapped inside, grated noisily down the incline. A rotor blade snapped off and went spinning away. A moment later a formation of up-jutting rocks caught the *Skeeter* like a giant outstretched hand.

The girls stared blankly at the wreckage, hoping against hope that Bud was still alive. As they waited,

A formation of up-jutting rocks caught the

frantic because they could not help, the seconds seemed like centuries.

Suddenly Sandy grabbed Phyl's arm. She had heard a faraway creaking sound. Slowly the twisted door of the helicopter was being forced open. Bud staggered out, seemingly uninjured. The girls called down to him.

"I feel like a one-wheeled tricycle," Bud replied. His voice was barely audible to the girls. "Pretty banged up but all in one piece."

Sandy and Phyl sighed in relief but their elation was short-lived. Bud was still trapped! Hanging precariously, halfway down the cliff, he could neither climb down nor locate any footholds for an ascent.

Bud, realizing the near futility of his situation, knew he must not become panicky.

Settling back against the helicopter, he surveyed the scene. A descent was out of the question. The cliff walls rose in a sheer line from the desert floor. One slip and he would be battered against broken boulders that fanned out at the base.

His only chance was to risk a climb. He would have to do it without the assistance of caulked climb-

Skeeter *like a giant outstretched hand*

ing shoes or a pickax. But one essential he could not do without was a rope.

Bud examined the wreckage for a rope, but there was none aboard. There were, however, control cables. These were built into the fuselage and ran from the cabin to the engine and rotors.

Reaching for the emergency tool kit, the pilot clipped long lengths of cable and spliced them together. It was a slow, drawn-out process. His hands were blistered and raw when he finished the final splice.

Using the cable as a lasso, Bud looped it around a projecting stone. Then, after filling his pockets with tools, he pulled himself up to a ledge a few feet above. From there he was able to risk throwing the line to Sandy. She leaned over the edge, with Phyl clutching her ankles.

Sandy missed the cable on the first toss but caught it on the second throw, and tied it around what seemed to be a rather firm pillar of stone. Bud gave the cable a few preliminary yanks. The stone crumbled.

"Wow!" he gasped as the pieces of rock fell past him.

The next time, the girls anchored the cable firmly around a deeply embedded boulder. The line held, and Bud, after wrapping it twice around himself, leaned back into space and began to pull himself upward.

Progress was slow and painstaking. Bud lifted one

foot cautiously above the other, swaying to maintain his balance. It was twenty minutes before he was safely beside the girls.

"Thank goodness!" both girls cried, hugging him in their relief.

Bud grinned, but he was too physically exhausted to make one of his usual wisecracks. It was many minutes before the full import of the situation dawned on them. Many hours would pass before they were reported missing and a rescue party sent after them.

"At least we're all safe," Sandy remarked philosophically.

"But the crows may return," Phyl said worriedly.

Bud shook his head hopefully. "I believe that they've done their work for today." He looked down at the badly mangled helicopter and thought of how close they had come to total disaster.

Their situation, nevertheless, was far from pleasant. They were without food or supplies. The chance of a stream on this barren mesa was nil. Should they have to remain past sundown, they would suffer from the night's intense cold, since they were not warmly dressed.

Bud, realizing the urgent need for psychology to keep the girls from becoming frightened, sprawled out casually on the ground and scooped up a handful of earth. "Do you think that the legend about buried Indian treasure on Purple Mesa could be true?" he mused aloud.

"I'm sure it is," said Sandy, brightening.

"The legend says its fabulous," Phyl added. "There are supposed to be hundreds of hand-carved necklaces, solid-silver brooches, and bracelets set with precious stones."

"Then let's start digging," Bud urged, relieved that he had been able to divert the girls' minds from their plight.

Phyl and Sandy eagerly discussed the most likely spot to search.

"If I were an Indian I'd bury the treasure near that fissure," said Bud, indicating an uneven crack in the ground. "That way I'd have a marker and know just where to find it."

Phyl did not agree. "No wise Indian would do that. It would be too obvious."

Using the tools Bud had taken from the helicopter, the trio began digging for the legendary treasure. Each one chose a different area to explore.

By midafternoon there were a dozen miniature foxholes on the mesa top. The girls were beginning to tire.

"Maybe we'd better rest for a time," Bud suggested.

"But we may never come here again," said Sandy. She tossed a scoopful of earth over her shoulder and continued to dig. "Think of all that treasure!" she said.

Bud grinned, shaking his head helplessly. "Carry on, girls. I'll just supervise for a while."

He sat on a flat rock and watched with mounting skepticism as the girls plowed up the surface of Purple Mesa. Suddenly a shriek of joy sent him leaping to his feet. Fifty yards away, Phyl was jumping up and down, shouting, "We found the treasure! We found it!"

Bud dashed over to where Sandy was holding an object aloft. After she had scraped the caked earth from it, Bud whistled in amazement. It was an ancient turquoise-and-silver ring!

"I can't believe it!" he said in astonishment. "Let me have one of those tools!"

In no time he too had forgotten that the trio were cut off from civilization. For hours the three clawed at the earth, digging one hole after another. The sky turned scarlet, then magenta. Finally the weary searchers were forced to give up as dusk came on. The treasure hunt was at an end with only one ring to reward their efforts.

Now Purple Mesa took on a rather eerie aspect as lengthening shadows of lavender and violet crept across its surface. Deeper purple hues cast an unreal pallor on their faces. The cold of the desert night began to make itself felt.

"If only we had a fire!" moaned Phyl, her teeth chattering.

"I'm getting hungry," Sandy said wistfully.

Bud remained silent. His eyes watched the ever-darkening skies for some hopeful sign of a rescuer.

"Tom will be here," he said. "When we don't re-

turn on schedule, he won't waste a minute in starting a search."

As the last ray of daylight filtered out, the powerful beams of the *Sky Queen's* landing lights appeared
on the horizon. The huge ship thundered toward
them until it was directly overhead. The Flying Lab
hovered over the mesa and began to descend.

The three marooned below waved frantically.
Tom, relieved to see them alive and safe, blinked
his lights in answer. He held the ship motionless in
the air, keeping the intense blast of the jet lifters
away from the trio on the mesa. Because of the fiery
blast, a landing would be impossible.

A solution to the rescue problem soon became ap-
parent to Tom. First he maneuvered the *Sky Queen*
over to the edge of the precipice and then slowly
permitted the ship to sink down until she was
slightly above the mesa top. The doors of the bay
were opened, and Sterling and Hanson hurled down
a flexible metal ladder. On the third try Bud caught
it and managed to hold it taut while first Phyl, then
Sandy, scrambled to the safety of the *Sky Queen*.

With no one to anchor the ladder, Bud realized
that as soon as his feet left the ground the ladder
would swing under the belly of the *Sky Queen* and
expose him to the intense heat and air blast of the
jet lifters. He wondered if he would be able to climb
up, hand over hand, fast enough to escape being
blown off the ladder. It was a chance he would have
to take.

Stepping onto the first rung, Bud felt the ladder swing forward. Quickly he reached up and grasped the next rung, and the next and the next.

"Hurry!" cried Sandy from the bay.

But speed on the twisting, swaying ladder was out of the question. It was all Bud could do to hang on. Terror in his eyes, he looked at the lifters.

The next moment, the ladder was swept toward the fiery blast!

CHAPTER 18

ROBOT TENNIS

TOM INSTANTLY REALIZED that only one course of action could save Bud—to put the *Sky Queen* into forward motion and cut off the lifters. But he must do it without the slightest jar or Bud would be flung off into space.

"Hang on, everybody!" he shouted through the loud-speaker system, switching off the lifters and easing the great ship into a slow, downward glide away from the mesa.

With hope in his heart he looked below. Bud was still hanging on! And the ladder was being pulled up at lightning speed by Sterling and Hanson. Tom set the plane on automatic pilot and raced to the Flying Lab's hangar. He was greatly relieved to find Bud there.

"Bud!" he cried. "Boy, am I glad to see you safely aboard!"

His sister was already insisting upon dressing Bud's injured hands, though the youth said that it wasn't necessary.

"Sandy's right," said Tom. "Go to the infirmary and get fixed up. Phyl, you come up front with Hank and Arv and me and tell us what happened."

When he heard the story Tom cried, "The crows again! Did any of you see a plane around from which the birds might have been controlled?"

Phyl shook her head. "There wasn't any as far as we could see."

"It must have been above the clouds," Hank offered, and since there was no other solution, they accepted this explanation.

Sandy and Bud joined the others then, commenting ruefully on the whole experience.

"And on top of everything else," Sandy said with disgust, "we found only this one ring out of all that legendary treasure!"

Tom grinned. "Too bad, Sis. Would you like to come back and try again?"

"No, thanks, Tom. I'm convinced now that there's more legend than treasure on Purple Mesa!"

Tom announced that in the morning they would try to rescue the *Skeeter*.

"We'll rig a winch and cable at the hangar doors. The wreckage can be secured with grappling hooks."

Directly after breakfast the next morning, Tom and his friends set out for Purple Mesa in the *Sky Queen*.

The winch-and-cable mechanism, rigged to avoid the jet lifters, projected on a boom out into space. Tom had to leave the hangar doors open, giving the usually graceful *Sky Queen* an ungainly appearance.

"What's worse," Bud complained, "it cuts down our speed and chances to maneuver. We're wide open to an assault."

Tom agreed that the device made the ship vulnerable. "We'll have to stand by with an ax to cut the mounting loose in case the crows attack."

But the ship was not molested. Reaching the cliffside, Bud took over at the controls. Tom insisted upon riding down on the cable to make an inspection of the *Skeeter* himself and attach the grappling hooks.

Grasping the metal ropes, his feet firmly planted in the clawlike hooks, he was lowered by Sterling while Hanson worked the winch. As he surveyed the badly damaged helicopter, which would need extensive repairs, the young inventor was beside himself with anger. Someday, he told himself, the scoundrel responsible for the savage attacks would be caught and punished by the law!

Moving about cautiously in order to keep his balance, Tom attached the grappling hooks to the *Skeeter*. He made sure that they were firmly secured, then signaled to the engineers above.

"Haul away!"

The derrick groaned, reduction gears spun, and the *Skeeter*, with Tom balancing on its roof, was lifted through the air. Once a strong wind current rocked it violently and Tom had to bear down heavily on a guy rope to keep from being tossed off.

The boom swung in. Tom ducked to miss the hangar ceiling and jumped off onto the deck.

The *Skeeter* was aboard and Tom was safe!

Bud piloted the *Sky Queen* back to the Citadel and set it down a few miles outside the enclosure.

Tom told the others that he would like to leave for Shopton that afternoon and asked them to be ready. "I've done all I can at this end of the line. The next job is giving my giant robots their final tests before shipping them out here."

Tom went off for a conference with his father before leaving. He found Mr. Swift in his office talking to Robert Turnbull. The latter seemed to be very upset.

"I—I don't know what you're talking about, Mr. Swift. I am in perfect health. I never felt better. I'm thoroughly calm, thoroughly calm."

Mr. Swift replied quietly, "It has always been the policy of my company to extend leave with full pay to any man involved in family stress. You say that no trace of your twin brother, Raymond, has been found. This naturally worries you. Why don't you take a vacation?"

"I'm sorry, Mr. Swift," replied the atomic scientist. "My work comes first. Things are at a critical stage here. I cannot shirk my part in it because of personal troubles."

There was further conversation but Robert Turnbull made it quite clear that he would not accept a vacation. He turned and left the room.

"Well, you have to give him *A* for loyalty," Tom remarked, then told his father of his plans to leave. "I'm sure that there won't be any trouble setting the other drone planes in flight when they arrive."

Mr. Swift smiled. "I'll feel a lot safer when they're at work, Tom. By the way, if you're satisfied with the tunnel, we'll line it with cement and put in the Tomasite-coated door to the basement."

"Everything's to specification, Dad. And I'll see you again in about two weeks."

"Fine, son," Mr. Swift said, clapping Tom on the back, "and in the meantime we'll try to track down the interference inside the plant that made Stan Lee topple over. Then, when you return, we can put the giant robots right to work."

The trip back to Shopton was uneventful. Tom and Sandy had dinner with their mother and spent the evening with her. Tom learned that Pins Zoltan had left the hospital and was in police custody. He had been subjected to intense questioning for over forty-eight hours by the police department's top crime probers, but had not cracked. There was no word on either Flash Ludens or Slick Steck. And Marco too was still unaccounted for.

"They're probably laying low getting ready to strike again," Tom thought but kept this worry to himself.

The following morning he moved into his private quarters which opened off the special testing laboratory at the Enterprises plant. For a week the youthful scientist buried himself in work, seeing no one but Chow. The cook hovered over Tom like a fretful hen, seeing to it that the absorbed young inventor had enough food and a proper amount of rest.

One afternoon Bud Barclay was startled to receive an intercom phone call from his friend. He was even more amazed when Tom asked:

"How about a robot game of tennis with me?"

"Have you gone off your rocker?" Bud cried.

Tom laughed. "Don't worry. I'm okay. My two giants are ready for a co-ordination test. I need your help."

"A game of tennis between two headless giants! This I want to see!" Bud howled. "I'll be right over."

When Bud arrived he found the two giants had temporary heads with antenna "hair" but the camera "eyes" were missing. Chow had dug up two rackets and carried them as the boys marched the two giant robots out of the building to a court behind the main offices.

Tom had arranged for two portable relotrol outfits, tuned to different frequencies, to be set up at each side of the court.

"My controls are going to have some pretty fast compensating to do." Bud grinned. "Score will be 6–0 in my robot's favor!"

"You're on!" Tom laughed as he placed his racket in the metal fingers of his robot. He eyed the windows behind them. "If my giant overcorrects," he warned, "we're in for some broken-window bills!"

"Toss you for first serve," Bud yelled, adjusting the magnitude-and-action blending controls. His robot took a vicious slash at the ball.

Tom laughed. "Net ball!"

The extraordinary sight drew a

His robot took a swing. The ball bounded back across the court. The game was on!

The extraordinary sight of two metal automatons, whacking a tennis ball, darting for rebounds, and charging the net, drew a large audience of plant workers. They cheered and whistled each time a ball was missed or a clever drive completed.

large audience of plant workers

"Brand my sunfishin' horse!" cried Chow. "This sure is the confoundinest game I ever did see!"

Tom's robot had trouble gauging the service line, while Bud's kept slamming out of the court on overhand returns. The boys' hands flew from hand control to foot angle directors and the robots' motors were constantly reversing.

At first the giants tended to exaggerate their motions, with the result that the game was clumsy and far from professional. As the game progressed, however, the automatons grew more adept and play became subtle and fine.

Suddenly Bud yelled, "Tom, this is for the time you took over Herbert in the skit!"

His robot drove a slashing ball to the corner of the court. Tom was unable to direct his robot to return it.

In the end, Bud's robot won the game, which had gone to deuce five times. Tom made his robot jump the net to congratulate the winning giant and the audience clapped in appreciation of the show.

Tom was pleased with the co-ordination of his metal men and told Bud only one thing remained to be done now before the giants would be ready for shipment to the Citadel.

"What's that?"

The inventor said that the television cameras, which would be the "eyes" of the robot to report what was happening inside the atomic energy plant, worked well enough under ordinary circumstances.

But the phosphors on the screens of the camera tubes were sensitive to the invisible but powerful radiation produced by the radioactive materials in the pile. This intense radiation would fog the picture on the iconoscope face and literally blind the robot.

Throughout the late afternoon and early evening, Tom labored over the problem. The cameras themselves were protected by asbestalon. The problem was how to keep the radiation from entering through the lens. A few experiments with filters proved fruitless.

Finally, the young inventor set up a series of mirror light baffles. These caught the visible light and reflected it into the tube while absorbing and deflecting the harmful radiation. Thus the screen was protected. After several hours of adjustments, the reflection principle was fully perfected!

Tom was now satisfied with the "eyes" of his robot. Excitedly he closed the laboratory with the thought of going home and telling his mother. She must be the first to know of his success!

As he started down the corridor he heard his telephone ring. Unlocking the door, he picked up the receiver.

A strained, faraway voice said, "Tom Swift?"

"Yes."

"This is Marco. Please," the man said in a pleading tone, "if you'll promise not to punish me, I'll lead you to the person who is back of all your troubles—the man who's after your robot."

CHAPTER 19

THE WATCHMAN'S
CONFESSION

THE UNEXPECTED WORDS of the night watchman startled Tom. Perhaps Marco was not a traitor after all!

"How soon can you be at my office?" Tom asked.

"I don't dare come to the plant, Tom," the trembling voice whispered in reply. "I'm afraid that someone might see me."

"Why did you spy against us, Marco?" Tom asked, trying to draw the elderly man out while he was in contact with him.

"He—he hypnotized me. He put me under a—a spell, so I had to help him."

"*Who* put you under a spell, Marco?"

"Please, Tom," the man pleaded. "I don't want to say any more over the telephone. I'm terribly afraid. I'm sorry if I've done you or your father any harm. I'll do anything to make it up."

Tom checked his wrist watch. "Go to the York Hotel in downtown Shopton," he instructed. "Take a room there and wait for me. I'll be up at eleven o'clock."

"Right, Tom. I'll do just that," the man promised.

Tom broke the connection and signaled the operator. In rapid order he placed a double-circuit call to Radnor on one line and Bud on another.

"I'm not absolutely sure that Marco is on the level," he said, after reporting his conversation with the watchman. "For all we know, it could be another ambush."

"Do you think they'd risk an attack on a crowded street?" Bud asked.

"I told Marco to take a hotel room," Tom replied.

"Just the same," Radnor broke in, "I wouldn't put anything past those bank robbers."

Tom arranged to have both Bud and Radnor follow him to the hotel.

"We'll meet a block away and you two amble along behind me," he instructed. "In that way we'll be ready for any attack."

The arrival was timed accurately and Tom's every move was covered precisely according to plan. There were no attempts on Tom during the walk to the York Hotel. He entered the lobby through a revolving door and reached the room-clerk's desk without being stopped.

Bud and Radnor followed him up a stairway to Marco's room but remained in the corridor. The security officer held the toe of one shoe against the door to keep it open a crack.

The guard was in tears and almost cringed as he began the tale of his misdeeds.

"He mesmerized me, that's what he did. Talked on and on in a low voice till he had me in a trance. I couldn't help carrying out his commands. When I started obeying him I couldn't stop. Till now, that is. I'm through with him."

"Who was this person?" Tom asked.

"Raymond Turnbull."

The escaped mental patient!

Marco continued, "He was waiting outside my house one night when I got home. I live alone, you know. He came every night after that and we talked. I'd get sleepier and sleepier.

"Somehow I fell under his power. Turnbull made me bring him the model of the Flying Lab, and he put the recording machine in it. Every night I'd change the tape. Sometimes I'd bring it to a boardinghouse. Other times I'd mail it to a box number. When Mr. Dilling called you about locating the shack, I overheard him and phoned Raymond at the boardinghouse."

"What's the address of the house?" Tom asked.

The old watchman thought for a moment. "I can't remember—I think it's Bond Street. But I can take you there. It's on the outskirts of town to the south."

"We'll go there at once," Tom decided.

When the two came out of the room, Bud and

Radnor were hidden in an alcove, but the shadowing arrangement continued as soon as they all left the hotel.

The watchman and Tom went directly to the neighborhood where the boardinghouse was located. At Bond Street they turned onto the quiet residential street.

Behind, Bud and Radnor kept a sharp lookout for signs of a trap. Bud was trailing in the shadows of trees and houses, while Radnor came up the block on the other side.

It was exceptionally dark and they had to depend on a few street lights, spaced at wide intervals, for illumination. Tom instinctively slowed down as he approached the house, which had a porch across the front. He listened carefully to judge when Bud and Rad would be in the best position to cover his entrance.

There was no sound except that of his friends' footsteps. Then the stillness was broken by a high-pitched scream. It seemed to have come from the boardinghouse toward which they were heading!

"It sounded like a woman!" Tom cried, then called, "Bud, you and Rad stay under cover till I signal you."

Bud and Radnor darted for concealment into some bushes across the street. They heard the front door of the boardinghouse slam shut and saw a porch light flash on.

A man began to pound on the door. His features

were clearly visible in the light. The next second Marco cried out:

"I know that man! He's one of the doctors from Blackstone."

The man heard him and turned to look. As Marco and Tom ran up, the doctor exclaimed, "Marco! What are you doing here?"

Stammering in confusion, Marco introduced Tom and Dr. Morrow and said they were looking for Raymond Turnbull.

"So am I," said Dr. Morrow. "The hospital finally traced him to this address, but when I spoke to the landlady, she became hysterical and shut the door in my face. She claims Turnbull's gone and she wants nothing to do with any more gangsters."

"Maybe I can help," Tom said. He rapped on the door and called out: "It's all right to let us in. This is Tom Swift of Swift Enterprises."

The woman peered at him from behind a curtain in the hall window. Then, evidently recognizing the young inventor from newspaper pictures, she opened the door and invited the callers into her living room.

Dr. Morrow introduced himself again and told why he had come. "Raymond Turnbull escaped from our mental hospital about a month ago," he said. "Will you please tell us what you know about him and where I may find him."

"I can't tell you where he is," said the woman, adding that her name was Mrs. Riley. She apologized for her hysteria and explained, "I've been terribly upset by what's happened. When Mr. Turnbull first took the room he told me he was a professor. I never paid much attention to him. He spent all his time with his papers and studies. I thought he was a fine gentleman.

"Then he began to have callers. One night a swarthy-looking man with a mustache came. I kept thinking he looked familiar. The next morning I remembered seeing his picture in a newspaper. He was a member of that Briggin gang. The one they call Slick."

Mrs. Riley held her handkerchief to her nose and began to sniffle. "Oh, I was so upset. I started to call the police. Just then, one of my other boarders told me he'd left in the middle of the night. Took all his things with him—even the funny tape machine he had. I was so relieved to have him gone that I didn't bother to notify the police."

Marco had begun to shake. It was evident that he had had no idea Raymond Turnbull was mixed up with bank robbers!

"Oh," the watchman wailed, "I never thought—"

He was interrupted by Tom, whose eyes were riveted on a metal picture frame that hung opposite one of the opened living-room windows. As he stared, the frame began to glow dimly with an orange light.

"Quick!" he cried, as the picture glass suddenly shattered with a loud crack. "Hit the floor, everybody!"

CHAPTER 20

THE MASKED INTRUDER

AS TOM SHOUTED the warning, he ducked below the window sash. Dr. Morrow followed suit. Marco and Mrs. Riley seemed flustered by Tom's sudden orders. The watchman lost his balance and sprawled aimlessly beneath a large oak table, while the woman froze, her eyes bulging at the sight of the orange light still playing on the picture frame.

"I think someone in the yard is trying to knock us out with a heat ray," Tom whispered. "Get down! Play dead!" He crumpled into an inert heap near the door, setting an example for the others.

The announcement was too much for the frightened landlady who immediately fainted, making the situation even more realistic. Marco and the doctor lay motionless.

Out of the corner of one eye, Tom watched the

front door. In a moment he heard a click and the door opened.

A masked man stood there. He was of medium height with dark hair. In one hand he carried what Tom assumed to be the knockout weapon—a monochromatic infrared beamer.

Stepping into the living room, he paused and surveyed the limp bodies. Apparently satisfied, he started for the stairway.

As soon as the masked intruder had vanished up the steps, Tom crawled along the floor to the front door. Cautiously he opened it. Luck was with him. The hinges did not squeak.

Tom reached for the flashlight in his pocket and held it at arm's length out the door. He blinked the beam three times in rapid succession. Then he sent three longer flashes, following these with three more short ones—the international signal of distress. He hoped Bud and Radnor were watching carefully and that they realized from the silence of his plea the need for extreme caution.

Tom left the door ajar, removed his shoes, and tiptoed to the stairway. He took each step with extreme care, knowing that one chance creak of a board and the intruder would come running and use the ray at close range.

"Who can he be?" Tom wondered. "Raymond Turnbull?"

Reaching the head of the stairs, he looked down

a narrow hallway. A few feet ahead of him the masked stranger was kneeling before a vent in the building's air-heating system. He had lifted the vent grill and was reaching inside, apparently groping for something.

The man withdrew his hand, obviously satisfied. By the hall light Tom could see that he was holding a small metal panel with a red button on it. Several wires dangled free at one end.

With the man intensely absorbed in the device and the beamer lying on the floor beside him, Tom knew this was the moment for action.

He leaped, caught the man off balance, and knocked him to the floor, rolling him away from the beamer. A scuffle followed, but finally both got to their feet. The masked man swung furiously at Tom and kicked him viciously.

Tom retaliated with three quick uppercuts that staggered his opponent. In desperation the man dived at Tom, slammed him against the banister, and lunged for the beamer.

Tom grabbed his ankles with a flying tackle that sent the masked man sprawling. Bud, with Radnor at his heels, charged up the stairs and grabbed the beamer while Radnor unmasked the man.

"Slick Steck!" Radnor cried.

While the prisoner glared in hatred at his captors, Steck was marched downstairs, where Mrs. Riley was being revived by Dr. Morrow. She opened her eyes and gazed in terror.

"Oh!" she screamed. "That's the man! It's that Slick fellow!"

"Start talking, Slick!" Radnor barked at the bank robber.

"I'm not saying a word," replied the man. "You've got nothing on me."

"Okay. We'll let the police do it." Tom turned away.

A cunning light came into the prisoner's eyes. "I might trade a little information for my freedom," he said. "Just what is it you're interested in finding out, Swift?"

"We're interested in all your dealings with Raymond Turnbull."

He expected the mention of the name to surprise the bank robber. Instead, Tom was the surprised one.

"Are you crazy?" Slick Steck snarled. "I haven't been working with Raymond Turnbull. You've got your names mixed. I've been—er—conducting business arrangements with the professor himself, *Robert* Turnbull."

The disclosure electrified his listeners. Before they recovered their composure, Steck continued.

"Sure I worked with the prof. It was a two-way venture. He was going to make bank robbing a safe and easy proposition for us—a sure thing. In return, the gang would take care of a few little matters for him, here in Shopton, while he was out of town on some other business."

"At the atom plant, no doubt," thought Tom.

Radnor prodded Steck with another question. "Just how would these holdups be accomplished?"

"With a robot," he replied. "It was going to be great. He promised to get us one of Tom Swift's robots. It would have a machine gun mounted on the end of one arm." Steck laughed hollowly. "The thing would have been rigged up like a walking tank. No bank-guard's bullets or tear-gas bombs could have stopped it. The robot would just walk right out with the money."

Tom, although enraged at this scheme, was intrigued by its ingenious idea. "Where was the robot going to be controlled from?"

Steck replied, "The whole operation would have been worked from an innocent-looking car."

"What about after the robbery?" said Bud. "Wouldn't the robot be followed?"

"Turnbull thought of everything," their prisoner explained. "The banks chosen to be robbed would always be near a river and the robot would disappear into the water and walk under the surface to a secret meeting place miles away. You know how fast those things can go if you want them to. Then he'd come up and we'd get the money."

Astounded at the disclosure, Tom felt that he should get in touch with his father at once. But first he must learn all he could from the prisoner.

"The prof was teaching my friends and me a lot of scientific stuff," said the ex-convict, smirking. "He showed us how to use all sorts of small machines like the monochromatic infrared beamer you took away from me. That gimmick I took out of the vent upstairs is a new type of electrical control button. A swivel switch, he calls it."

Tom examined the gadget. Its sliding segment enabled the single button to do the work normally accomplished by an entire bank of toggle switches.

"I was supposed to hold on to it until Turnbull came to my house," Steck explained.

"And just where is that?" asked Radnor.

The gangster grew sullen. "I've told you all I'm going to tell you."

"Why did you tell us this much?" Bud asked, puzzled.

Steck was silent for a few seconds. Then he took a deep breath. "The reason I told you all this," he said, "is because you got nothing to hold me on. And furthermore, I'm through with Robert Turnbull. I think the guy's nuts. He's got a twin who's crazy, but I think Robert's worse."

CHAPTER 21

TWIN TROUBLE

THE POLICE were summoned by Radnor. Manacled and snarling, Slick Steck was taken by them to the Shopton jail. After they had gone, Bud turned to Tom.

"I don't get this about Robert Turnbull," he said. "You and your father thought he was perfectly sane, didn't you?"

"Yes, Bud, and that gives me an idea," said Tom. He turned to Marco. "Did you ever see Mr. Raymond Turnbull's twin brother?"

"Yes. Once about eight months ago when I was working at Blackstone. He came to visit Raymond. He's an identical twin."

"Then the man you thought was Raymond could have been Robert?" Tom asked.

"Oh, no. I couldn't be fooled. Anyway, Raymond talked about things that happened at Blackstone that his brother wouldn't know."

"Then there's only one answer," Tom said. "Raymond must be impersonating his brother to avoid detection. The Briggin gang doesn't know that Robert is engaged in secret work at our atomic plant, so they wouldn't suspect Raymond's impersonation."

Dr. Morrow nodded. "And Raymond, as Robert, would not be in danger of being sent back to Blackstone."

"He even fooled the Briggin gang," Radnor added.

"It's tragic the way a fine mind will snap under the pressure of overwork," Tom remarked.

The doctor placed a hand on Tom's shoulder and said in a serious voice, "Raymond Turnbull's confinement at Blackstone was not due to overwork."

"What do you mean?"

"Well, his condition is one we run into quite often at the hospital. It developed like this. Raymond once made some incorrect calculations in a nuclear experiment, an understandable mistake in research of such a crucial nature.

"On the basis of that error a fellow physicist brought together a near-critical mass of plutonium, and, as a result, was subjected to radiation. Fortunately he recovered. However, Raymond, an extremely sensitive person, felt totally responsible and brooded over it so much that his mind snapped."

"Why didn't we hear any news of his escape?" Radnor asked.

"Because of the top-secret work he was doing prior

to his misfortune, our search for Raymond has been carried on without any publicity," the doctor replied.

"And would this condition explain his recent criminal associations?" Tom queried.

"It's very likely," Dr. Morrow answered. "Physicians can never predict to what lengths such an obsession will drive a person. Almost any action is possible."

After a pause the doctor added, "I hope that you people will help the hospital authorities find this patient before he carries out the dire schemes we overheard him planning while he was at Blackstone. Oh, one thing I didn't make clear. His case isn't hopeless, but he needs further care and treatment."

"We'll sure do our best to find him," declared Bud, memories of his experience on the mesa still fresh in his mind.

Wishing to communicate with his father at once and give him the complete story, Tom said good-by to the others and went to his office. There he called the Citadel and gave Mr. Swift the full details.

The elder scientist was grave, remarking that the situation called for extreme care. Raymond Turnbull's actions would doubtless be cunning and unpredictable.

"I'll have another talk with Robert Turnbull," he told his son. "It's possible that Raymond may communicate with him. I must admit, Tom, I won't feel comfortable until he's back at Blackstone."

"Do you think we should delay putting the pile into operation until we do know where he is, Dad?"

"I can't do that, Tom. It may be months or years before Raymond is located, and we can't postpone the official opening." Then he changed the subject, asking, "In the morning, will you find out about the two cybernetic arms and hands that are scheduled for shipment out here tomorrow?"

Mr. Swift was referring to the large mechanical sets which he had designed himself for use at the Citadel. Compared to similar ones on the market, however, these were smaller and lighter, yet equally dexterous. They would be suspended from an overhead rail at the point where radioactive slugs came from the oven. The hands would seize and pile them, ready for processing by Tom's giant robot.

"I'll do it first thing tomorrow," Tom promised.

At ten the next morning he was calling back. "Dad, the sets are being loaded on two planes right now," he reported.

The cargo ships were warming up on separate runways. The second set of the mechanical arms and hands was being run out to its plane on a flatcar.

"Take-off time is in ten minutes," Tom told his father. "Slim Davis is piloting one plane, Binky Jones the other."

"I'll keep in touch with them," said Mr. Swift, signing off.

After the take-off, Tom went to his lab to make final adjustments to the lens mirrors of the giant robot's camera "eyes." It was midafternoon when Mr. Swift radioed his son that the cargo planes were overdue.

"Our radio operator here lost contact with them over an isolated area," he reported, giving Tom the location. "I'm afraid they're in trouble."

Tom went into action. Picking up the intercom, he called Bud, Sterling, and Hanson.

"I'm taking off on a search flight," he told them. "How about meeting me at the *Sky Queen* and going along?"

Hank Sterling and Bud were at the Flying Lab's hangar five minutes after the report had been received. The ground crew, following a prearranged emergency procedure, had the ship fueled, above-ground, and ready for a take-off. When Tom and Hanson arrived, the young inventor explained to the others the reason for the hurried trip and added:

"I have the exact position of the missing planes at the time contact was broken." He held up a map. "The tower has marked the beam they were supposed to follow after that point."

"I'll call the tangents, boy," Bud offered, swinging up through the belly hatch of the Flying Lab.

Sterling and Hanson took observational posts, while Bud plotted the route that would carry them along the precise course taken by the missing aircraft.

Tom gave the elevators a quick lift. This was no time for gentle flight maneuvering. Tom was in a hurry and called upon the *Sky Queen* for every bit of thrust its engines possessed. Pushed to the limit, the Flying Lab shrieked across the sky at more than twelve hundred miles an hour.

This rate of speed was maintained until they approached the locality from which the cargo planes had last reported. Here Tom throttled back while the observers scanned the terrain with high-powered binoculars.

The land was desolate. Several times the intent group thought they had the planes spotted. But upon descending for a closer look, they discovered that shadows from rock formations were what had fooled them.

Almost at the point of discouragement, Bud suddenly spotted a sight that left no doubt in his mind. A silver "T," formed by the wings and fuselage of one of the cargo planes, was bobbing up and down in his binoculars.

"There's one of them, Tom!" he called excitedly. "Move in for a better look."

The lifters dropped them to within five hundred feet of the ground. Below was a scene that made the Swift group gasp angrily. One of the mechanical hand-and-arm sets was being loaded aboard a trailer truck by a group of men. They were working with great haste, gesturing and glancing up constantly at the huge *Sky Queen* now threatening overhead. Other men were backing a cab up to the trailer.

"They're stealing it!" Hank shouted.

"Not for long!" said Tom.

The Flying Lab shifted its position until it was hovering directly over the men on the ground. Tom released the throttle. Blasts of flame and heat poured

Before the men had recovered from the first attack,

from the jet lifters, scattering the men before a withering rain of exhaust.

At the same time, the plane shot up a thousand feet. Before the group on the ground had recovered from the first attack, Tom was dropping down for a second try at scaring them off. This time the drivers and their helpers scrambled for the cab and raced away over the desert, abandoning the trailer, the stolen cargo, and the plane.

a second blast of flame poured from the jet lifters

"We did it!" Bud chortled.

Rather than pursue the thieves, Tom decided to land and search for a trace of the pilot and crew. The *Sky Queen* came to rest in a large open space near the trailer. Hanson and Sterling darted over to inspect the mechanical arm. The set seemed none the worse for having been moved.

Meanwhile, Tom and Bud went ahead to the plane. "It's Jones' ship," Tom said, noting the serial number on the wing.

An ominous silence hung over the area. There was not a single sound from the plane.

"Where's the pilot?" Bud asked fearfully. "And what's happened to the crew?"

CHAPTER 22

A CLEVER FOIL

THE HATCH of the cargo plane gaped open and the loading ramp was down. Tom and Bud hurried inside, going at once to the control cabin. The pilot was not there.

"Bud, look!" Tom cried, pointing to a pair of earphones. "They're stained with blood!"

Worried, the two boys rushed to the navigator's compartment. Scuff marks on the floor indicated that someone had been dragged out the door.

Tom and Bud separated and made a frantic search of the plane. In the main cargo hold, Tom found the limp body of Jones sprawled out, face down. Near him lay the other two members of the crew.

At this moment Bud rushed in. "Are they—"

Tom was already examining Jones. To the inventor's relief, the pilot was breathing, though his pulse was slow. A huge lump near the base of his skull gave mute evidence of a vicious blow.

"He's alive, thank goodness," Tom reported to Bud, who was kneeling beside one of the other men.

"This fellow too," Bud said.

The third crew member was also found to be alive. All three had been cracked on the head from behind.

"We'd better carry them to the *Sky Queen*," Tom suggested.

Gently they lifted Jones first and carried him out of the compartment and down the ramp. Arv Hanson and Hank rushed up to offer assistance.

"Hurry and bring out the other two in the cargo compartment," Tom instructed. "I don't know how badly they're injured."

Five minutes after the men had been laid on cots in the *Queen*'s infirmary, they opened their eyes and looked about. Jones was the first to speak.

"It must have been a stowaway," he explained. "I didn't see his face. Heard footsteps coming up behind. Turned to look and everything went black."

Tom wondered whether the stowaway had been someone working at Enterprises or an outsider who had managed to slip aboard the plane. Bud ventured a guess that it had been Raymond Turnbull or a member of the Briggin gang working under him.

"Tom gave the guys who tried to steal the arm gadget a good scare with the jets," Bud told Jones. "I don't think they'll try another attack."

When the other two men revived, they insisted

upon continuing the flight. Tom, hoping they would be all right, gave an okay but insisted that Hank go along to help pilot the cargo ship.

With Arv Hanson and Bud he watched it take off. Then the three re-entered the Flying Lab, eager to pursue their search for the other missing plane.

A wide sweep of the skies covered many additional square miles of open land, but there was no sign of the lost ship.

As Tom was about to give up hope, an S O S crackled in over the Swift wave band. The call was from Slim Davis. He was down a hundred miles to the southwest of Tom's present position.

"There's a prisoner—" he began. Then the sound faded and Tom could not rouse the sender.

"It's Slim! He has a prisoner!" Tom shouted to his friends in the *Sky Queen*. As the Flying Lab flew to the rescue, speculation ran high as to who it might be.

The cargo plane was sighted in a pasture several miles from a small farming community. This time there were no men or trucks surrounding it. Slim waved Tom on and the Flying Lab glided in without using the lifters.

"We were too fast for the stowaway," Slim told Tom. "He surprised the copilot and me from behind and rapped Jack with a monkey wrench. But when he swung at me I banked the plane and he hit the instrument panel instead. It crippled us and we were forced to land."

"Where's the stowaway and who is he?" Tom asked eagerly.

"He wouldn't give his name. I tied him up and we called the local police from a farmhouse. They haven't come yet."

Slim led the Swift group to the cargo compartment. Lacking rope, he had bound the intruder with wire. The man's hair, mussed in the scufffle, had fallen forward, revealing a jagged scalp scar.

"Flash Ludens!" Tom exclaimed as the man glared at him.

Bud chortled gleefully. "So the Briggin gang is running out of top men!" he taunted.

The bank robber glowered. "Just what are you talking about?"

"You don't have to play foxy with us, Flash," Tom replied. "Slick Steck has already confessed. We know all about your gang's setup."

Ludens listened to Tom's story of the tie-in between the Briggin gang and Raymond Turnbull, first with disbelief, then with a growing sense of defeat.

"All right, Swift," he growled. "So we have been working with Prof Turnbull. He helps us. We help him. This job was his idea."

"What was the reason?"

"To delay the opening of your atomic energy plant. He didn't tell us why."

"Where is Turnbull now?" Tom queried.

"I don't know."

Flash Ludens refused to say any more about Turnbull, so Tom changed his line of questioning. "Who was the stowaway on the other plane?" he asked.

"I got a pal of mine to work the job. If you want to know who he is, find him," the prisoner sneered.

Though he did not expect to receive an answer to the question, Tom was about to ask how the stowaways had slipped into the Enterprises grounds, when Flash Ludens burst into a raucous laugh.

"Getting into your place was so easy it makes a bank job seem really tough," he bragged. "One of those tape recordings told what day those arms were going to be shipped. So my pal and I—we studied all your workmen and picked out two that looked enough like us to fool the gatemen. This morning we just conked 'em in a lonely spot and took their credentials. No trouble at all getting in."

The inventor and his friends looked at one another. Admittance to the plant from now on was going to be double-checked!

A few minutes later the police arrived and arrested Flash Ludens. The country officers seemed overawed to be in charge of such a famous underworld character. After they had gone, Tom, using the facilities of the shop aboard the Flying Lab, repaired the crippled cargo ship's instrument panel. The plane then went on to its destination. This time both cargo ships reported in and the mechanical arms were safely delivered to the Citadel.

By phone Mr. Swift told Tom he had checked and

rechecked security at the plant. There was no leak. The reason Stan Lee had fallen must have been because of a fault in the control system. Tom flew out there at once in a jet to test the small robot again. It worked perfectly!

"I can't understand what happened before," he told his father, puzzled about the whole episode.

He returned to Shopton and immediately began putting the final touches on his giants' heads. When the two robots were completely assembled and ready for work, he called Chow in.

"You get the first view, 'pardner,'" Tom said to him.

The Texan stared, speechless. He wagged his head and scratched his bald spot. At last he said:

"Tom, these here are too human lookin' for comfort. Why, brand my cow skulls, that giant's actually eyin' me!"

In each "eye socket" Tom had fitted a lens for the two television cameras. Below them and centered in the nose position, Tom had mounted the forward transmitting antenna. For a mouth, the giant had a rectangular-hinged panel, which, when opened, showed several knurled knobs for making adjustments in the electrical circuits within the robot's body.

"An' look at those lil ole ears!" Chow marveled. "Kin he hear with 'em, Tom?"

"He sure can." The inventor laughed. "They're microphones."

These sensitive, multidirectional installations bulged from baffle enclosures on both sides of the head.

"There's just one thing missing, Tom," said Chow. "Hair. The giant's balder'n I am. Not a hair on his head."

Tom grinned. "That's right. And he won't miss them any more than you do."

"When are you takin' this fella out West?"

"After I give him one more test—the test of fire. Chow, you're invited to a little ceremony tomorrow afternoon to watch it."

"I'll be there. I sure wouldn't miss it. Not for all the longhorns in Texas!"

Tom spent the rest of the day preparing for the test. A special glass furnace, in which the giant would perform his inventor's every command, had been constructed in one of the sheds. It stood at the end of a ramp up which the robot would walk. Set some distance back from the furnace and behind a glass partition was a low, portable control board. Banked on each side of it were seats for the audience.

Following a luncheon at the plant, with Chow in charge, Mrs. Swift, Sandy, Phyl, the cook, and Tom's engineering staff filed into the shed and took seats.

"This is like going to the theater," said Phyl. "Tom, when do the actors come on?"

"Right now. Mother, are you ready?"

"Mother?" Sandy echoed, puzzled.

Mrs. Swift and her son merely smiled. As Tom

threw a switch, the relay panels lighted up. Next, the young inventor set the circuit switches to start the action tapes.

A thunderous rapping was heard on the corrugated steel door that formed one side of the platform. A moment later the door rolled into the roof and the giant robot clumped in.

"Tom, he's marvelous!" Sandy exclaimed, as the giant took the center of the stage and stood facing his audience.

Mrs. Swift left her seat and ascended the three steps at one end of the platform. Walking over to the giant, she reached up and touched his chest. In a clear voice she said:

"Since you stand for both atom and robot, I name you Ator!"

The audience applauded as she descended the steps.

"My second giant," Tom announced, "will be called Sermek in honor of the field of servomechanics."

Mrs. Swift now walked to the relay panel and pushed the button that would open the door to the furnace.

As the fierce heat waves began to billow over the platform, Ator marched forward into the roaring inferno. Every person in the shed leaned forward tensely.

Would Ator "live" or "die"? Would Tom's invention be a success?

CHAPTER 23

TRIAL BY FIRE

ATOR STRODE back and forth inside the furnace, looking like a giant knight in armor. Jets of chemical fire deluged his Tomasite-protected body, but not once did he waver or display a defect.

"I can hardly believe what I'm looking at," said Mrs. Swift, smiling proudly at her son.

As he directed Ator, Tom began addressing his audience through a small microphone hanging on his chest. "One task the robot will be called upon to do inside the atomic energy plant will be to replace neutron-soaking rods. I'll have him show you an example by using two ordinary metal batons—one used, one new."

The used rod lay in a groove on a steel shelf in the furnace. The other was on the floor.

Ator stooped over and the fingers of one hand came up with the new rod. In a deft movement with his other hand he lifted the old one out of place, dropped it into a basket, and carefully fitted the new rod into the groove.

"Well, brand my lariat!" Chow called out. "That sure was a neat trick."

Tom, his eyes twinkling, directed the robot to pick up both batons and twirl them in the manner of a drum major. The intricate juggling was climaxed by a series of tossing spins through the flames. The audience was in an uproar of praise and laughter. Tom himself was pleased at the degree of speed and accuracy with which the robot performed.

"Ator will now demonstrate his artistic ability," he announced, smiling. "As big chief of the atomic pile, he will be called upon to coat some of the equipment from time to time with rustproof paint."

Pretending to address his remarks to the robot, Tom instructed him to pick up a bucket of paint and a brush that stood near him.

"Start painting," the young inventor commanded, at the same time manipulating the controls for vertical arm strokes.

With total disregard for the fire, Ator began to cover the glass-brick wall that faced his audience.

"That's enough," said Tom. But Ator continued to paint. "Hey," the boy chided, "you're painting out the window! We can't see you."

The onlookers laughed as Tom allowed his giant robot to paint himself out of view as a climax to the performance. Then Ator opened the door and stalked onto the platform.

The plant engineers were enthusiastic in their praise and asked Tom how soon the giant would be shipped to the Citadel. In a hushed voice Tom replied:

"For security reasons I'm letting it be known that Ator and Sermek will leave next week. Actually they're going tonight. The moving will be done secretly and without lights."

Fortunately, the evening sky was brilliant with stars, and when the workers' eyes became accustomed to the dim light, they were able to load the *Sky Queen* quickly. Besides the two giant robots, they lifted aboard a huge square box fitted with metal straps.

Chow chortled. "So those mee-chanical guys travel with a trunk, eh? What kind o' gear's in it, Tom?"

"Actually it *is* gear," the young inventor replied. "The trunk contains Sermek's control panel. Ator's is already out at the Citadel."

"I see," said Chow, but shook his head uncomprehendingly.

When everything was in place, Tom summoned Bud, Radnor, Hank, and Arvid for the take-off. It was accomplished without fanfare and hours later they were circling over the Citadel, awaiting landing instructions.

"I see all the drone planes are at work," Bud remarked, watching the six automatic planes circling, ready to capture and guide in any unwanted visiting ship. They could also intercept any bomb that might be dropped, so that it would explode in the air, not on the ground.

"I'll feel a lot safer here now," Tom said quietly, recalling his narrow escape from the tunnel during his first visit.

"Me too," Bud said. "The drones will keep crows away, I suppose."

"Let's hope so, pal."

A hard-surfaced area had been marked out in red lights within the huge reserve as a landing mat for the *Sky Queen*. Tom guided the ship down, using the jet lifters cautiously to avoid jarring his valuable cargo.

Mr. Swift was waiting for the group as they climbed down from the plane. "Thank goodness you made it safely, Tom. After Jones' and Davis' experience, I was worried."

"Any more crows around?" his son asked.

"No, and I hope the capture of Flash Ludens has ended that trouble."

Tom inquired about Raymond Turnbull. Mr. Swift shook his head, saying, "His brother has become moody over the situation. Robert has been keeping irregular hours, coming in at odd times and staying away from here for long stretches on and off."

"Has it affected his work?" Tom questioned.

"I think not. But then everything is about ready for putting the pile into action. Opening ceremonies will take place two days from now, providing your robot and the relotrol are in working order."

"They are, Dad. Come and meet Ator and Ser-mek."

He escorted his father into the Flying Lab's hangar where the two giants stood, trussed with guy ropes to keep them from falling.

The sight of Ator and Sermek amazed even the seasoned inventor.

"It's an achievement to be proud of, son," he beamed. "I can hardly wait to see them in action. We'll have a test early tomorrow."

When the young inventor awoke the next morning in his bunk in the *Sky Queen,* the first rays of the desert sun were glinting into the cabin. Tom jumped up and went to make sure that Ator and Sermek were all right. Finding them still in position, he went to put on work clothes.

Directly after breakfast, the Citadel became a scene of excited anticipation. Crews had moved the two giant robots to a position between the control house and the outdoor shaft that led to the pile's tunnel entrance. A crowd of engineers had gathered to see them.

Meanwhile, Tom had made a final inspection of the relay panel in the double-walled passage surrounding the pile and the panel in the control house. Everything seemed to be in perfect working order.

Tom now gave instructions for the outdoor demonstration area to be cleared. The engineers spread out around the section, eagerly awaiting the test.

"Where's Robert Turnbull?" Tom asked his father, who was standing near the tunnel entrance. "I thought he'd want to watch the demonstration."

Mr. Swift looked about and shrugged. "Robert was around earlier. I know he wants to be on hand. He'll probably show up in a few minutes."

But the scientist did not put in an appearance. Finally Mr. Swift told Tom to proceed without him.

Tom walked to the control house, announcing that he would put Ator through a series of maneuvers such as he would perform in servicing the pile. The simplest movements would come first.

He had Ator stride up and down, bend, and stretch. Next, the giant picked up a steel bar and bent it easily in his great metallic fingers.

"What power!" exclaimed one of the technicians.

"I'd hate to have Ator get mad at me!" another said. "He'd crush you in nothing flat!"

Mr. Swift, who was still standing near the tunnel entrance, was pleased with the demonstration. He was about to walk to the control house and ask Tom to speed up Ator's actions when he noticed that the door to the tunnel's cargo elevator was open but the elevator was not at ground level.

"Ator may walk in there and tumble," the scientist said to himself, hurrying to close it. "What careless person left that door open?"

Tom and Bud in the control house saw him move toward the door, but the next instant were diverted by an unexpected sight. Ator had collapsed!

"What happened?" cried Bud.

"I don't know. The power's still on. The trouble must be in the tapes."

Disheartened, Tom was about to click off the controls when Ator revived. Getting up, the giant weaved clumsily for an instant, then started to run toward Mr. Swift.

The technicians shouted cries of warning to Mr. Swift as Tom fought frantically with the controls.

But the giant robot seemed to have developed a mind of his own!

In a moment his great legs had carried him to Mr. Swift's side. Ator pounced upon the inventor and seized him between his massive hands.

"Stop him! Stop him!" the onlookers screamed, rushing forward to help.

Desperately Tom tried to cut the power supply, but to no avail. Ator continued his devilish work. Holding his captive high overhead, he waved him back and forth.

Bud had raced from the control house to help the technicians who were attempting to knock down the giant. But Ator remained upright, keeping his balance, despite the combined weight pushing against him. Several men jumped into the air trying to grab Mr. Swift, but none of them could reach him. The robot held on tightly.

By this time, Ator was beginning to close both arms around his helpless victim. That viselike grip, Tom knew, would crush his father!

CHAPTER 24

THE GIANTS CLASH

IN DESPERATION Tom abandoned his struggle to control Ator, realizing there was only one remaining chance: Sermek!

Turning to the second robot's warmed-up control panel, he sliced down a series of knife switches, spun the dials, and Sermek strode into action, bearing down upon the first giant robot.

Ator seemed to sense the impending danger. The mechanical giant clanked to a halt, lowered his captive, and relaxed the iron-clad grip. Struggling to release himself, Mr. Swift fell free and scrambled to his feet. Bud was there instantly to help him to safety.

Turning, Ator advanced toward Sermek and the automatons circled each other warily. Ator's right hand contracted into the equivalent of a fist and his arm stiffened into a lance. He charged as Sermek braced his feet against the earth.

The giants collided with a crash that resounded deafeningly through the grounds. Tom fully realized the gravity of the situation. The hidden hand manipulating Ator seemed bent on an all-out battle without regard for the possible destruction of both robots. Somehow he must deactivate Ator's controls without permanent injury to either robot.

Ator backed off and began to stalk his opponent, looking for an opening. Then, pivoting quickly, he lunged forward. Sermek side-stepped, but not far enough to avoid a smash in the face that damaged his control circuits, stiffening the joints in one leg. The robot jockeyed awkwardly for position. Two more blows shook his eye circuits.

Tom worked feverishly to compensate for the distortion. If Sermek was to win now, Tom knew, the battle would have to end rapidly.

He switched to wrestling techniques. A clanging din filled the air as each giant fought for a hold on the other's vulnerable head mechanism. A contest of strategy, not strength, was exactly what Tom wanted. Now he could use scientific tactics based on his knowledge of the robot's structural operations.

For a moment Ator had the advantage. He broke a full nelson with a thrust that sent Sermek reeling back against the plant wall. But Sermek recovered quickly and sprang forward again. Leaping into the air, he lunged at Ator, and with one hand, short-circuited the receiving antenna atop the giant's head. Ator crashed to the ground.

Sermek had won!

Tom flung open the control-house door and dashed out. Ator's temporary master might have taken over the controls at the relay board and television screen in the plant. Racing past the fallen robot, he slipped through the milling crowd of workers and entered the double-walled enclosure which housed the long relay board. Abruptly Tom stopped in his tracks. Bud was coming down the passageway, weaving from side to side.

"Bud, what—"

"Electric shock," his friend panted, leaning against the wall for support. "I just came to. Knocked me out."

"Take it easy, Bud," Tom said. "Are you all right now?"

"Yes. But listen, Tom," he gasped. "On a hunch, I went to see if anyone was tampering with the relay panel. I saw Robert Turnbull at the controls just as I turned into the corridor! Then the shock hit me and I blacked out."

"Robert Turnbull!" Tom exclaimed. "Are you sure?"

"Positive, Tom!"

"Let's have a look at the relay panel," Tom said quietly.

The boys found a small secondary control board wired into the main panel feed line. A single shunt enabled its operator to disconnect Tom's wiring and substitute his own, completely by-passing the control-house wires. The evidence against Turnbull was overwhelming. Tom immediately ordered a building-by-building search. But the scientist had completely disappeared. Meanwhile, Radnor called a security-police conference to outline a plan of action. With no idea where Turnbull would strike next, every precaution had to be taken to protect the plant.

"We'll need a key man at each vital point," Radnor said. "Hank will watch the entrance gate. Arvid Hanson can guard the robots. I've already alerted the radar technicians to put a double watch on the patrolscopes."

Mr. Swift suggested that he remain in the control house to work the robots if the need arose.

While the men completed their plans, Tom, who had been deep in thought, startled the group by suddenly remarking, "I don't think that I've ever met the real Robert Turnbull. I think that Raymond— not Robert—has been working for us, here, for the past few weeks at least."

"What makes you think that?" Radnor asked in amazement.

"It all begins to tie in, Rad," Tom replied. "For instance, it explains Stan Lee's mysterious failure on that first test run out here and the way our enemies always knew our plans in advance, even after we discovered the recorder in the Flying Lab model."

"I agree, Tom," Mr. Swift said. "Raymond, passing successfully as his brother, probably used your stolen relotrol to take over Stan Lee's controls. And I think we can assume he intercepted Hanson's clearance papers. It probably was just another attempt to disrupt plant operations."

"Then what has happened to Robert Turnbull?" Radnor asked.

"Raymond might be holding him a prisoner," Tom replied. "And there aren't many places around here where he could be hiding him. Better check in town first, Rad. Meanwhile, I'll brief Dad on the robot controls."

After the men had left to take their appointed stations, Radnor telephoned the small hotel in town. He gave the clerk a description of Turnbull and asked if such a person was registered there. He was told that no one answering the description had taken a room. Further checking failed to provide a single lead in the small town.

Tom returned from the robot-control house and suggested that Bud and Radnor go with him on a search flight through the surrounding territory. Maps were checked for likely hide-outs in the vicinity. The mesa area with its natural crevasses and rock formations seemed the most logical starting point for the hunt.

With Tom at the controls, the Flying Lab was airborne fifteen minutes after a decision had been reached on the route they would take. Rad sat in the cockpit with Tom, while Bud stationed himself in the navigation dome. Soon a familiar view loomed ahead. They were approaching Purple Mesa.

"There's the old 'crows' nest,'" Bud called.

Tom reached for binoculars and scanned the face of the mesa closely. "You may have something there," he said.

The young inventor switched on the jet lifters and slowly guided the *Sky Queen* alongside Purple Mesa, approaching it from an unfamiliar angle.

"Well, will you look at that!" Bud yelled incredulously.

Directly before them was the entrance to an immense natural cavern, protected by overhanging boulders. The cave seemed to tunnel back from a large outcropping stone lip on which a midget black helicopter rested. Before Tom and his group had time to decide on a course of action, a flock of mechanical crows swarmed out of the cave and swung into formation over the Flying Lab.

One crow broke from the echelon and bore down in a screaming dive toward the mid-section of the huge plane. Its tremendous impact shook the fuselage, and the crow shattered in all directions against the *Queen*'s Tomasite covering. The rest of the flock attacked simultaneously, crashing into the wings and cabin. The great ship shivered but held steady. A second flock of mechanical missiles zoomed out of the cave at high speed. In rapid succession they slammed into the ship, battering themselves to pieces. The attack ended as abruptly as it had begun.

"Either they've run out of crows or they decided not to waste any more on us," Tom remarked.

"I bet they've thrown everything they had at us," Bud said. "Now let's get them!"

Radnor took over the controls and held the plane motionless at the edge of the shelf. Tom and Bud dropped a rope ladder and lowered themselves carefully to the rocky table. Tom cautiously entered the cave, Bud at his heels. The limestone interior was illuminated by incandescent lamps recessed in the cave walls. The boys continued on, following the lights, and soon found themselves in a passageway. After a short distance it turned abruptly and Tom and Bud stood before a rack of electronic controls.

"Seems to be a transmitter," Bud whispered. "But part of it looks something like your relotrol."

Tom nodded grimly and signaled to go on. They passed the control board and entered a large irregular cavern. About one third of the stone room was filled with a Diesel engine, a generator, and a large fuel-storage tank. On workbenches were various parts used in assembling the mechanical crows.

" 'Crows' nest' is right!" Bud whispered. "What a layout! But how did they get all this equipment in here?"

"I'd guess they dismantled it and ferried the sections in by helicopter," Tom said. "But where's the crows' owner? *Somebody* sent out those mechanical birds to attack us!"

"Do you think it's a trap?"

"We'll soon know, Bud. Come on, and be ready for trouble."

Leaving the machine-equipped area, they entered a dead-end room and found themselves face to face with the Turnbull twins!

One stood there, triumphant, with arms crossed and a wild, gloating look in his eyes. The other, haggard and drawn, was chained to the wall of the cave. On a table in front of them was an odd-looking mechanical gadget which Tom eyed with distrust.

For a moment no one moved. Then Tom approached the gaunt prisoner.

"Robert," he said gently, "I'm Tom Swift."

The man looked up at Tom with pleading eyes. "You should never have come here," he gasped.

"What do you mean?"

Robert strained against his bonds. "Tom," he warned frantically, "my brother plans to destroy the atomic energy plant and do away with you and your father."

Raymond's eyes gleamed in the glaring light. "I'll ruin all of them—the Swifts, the physicists too!" His voice rose to a screech. "I'll smash the atom smashers. Ha! That's pretty good! I'll turn the Citadel back into atoms. Nothing but atoms." He advanced menacingly toward Tom. "The atomic plant's as good as wrecked, Swift. The damage to the thermopile has already been done. I've seen to that. It will blow up six hours from now!"

Tom, looking sideways at Bud, said calmly, "Maybe there was an outfield error in your calculations, professor!"

Bud instantly interpreted the phrase as the code for "Grab this guy!" Both boys closed in on Raymond as he reached toward the switch of the machine on the table.

"When this switch is pulled it will blow up the whole cave and end it for all of us!" he screamed.

CHAPTER 25

ATOR'S TRIUMPH

AS RAYMOND reached for the switch, Tom and Bud dived at him. The screaming scientist toppled back, missing the fatal switch by inches! A moment later they had overpowered him. Tom found a set of keys and quickly released Robert Turnbull.

Rather than take the chance that the scientist would reach for the switch again, Bud and Tom manacled Raymond with the chains he had used to imprison his brother.

"We don't have much time," Tom warned. "Let's get to the plant, quick!"

They half pushed, half dragged the unwilling Raymond through the caverns until they reached the outer ledge. Bud helped Robert climb the dangling ladder to the *Sky Queen*. Then, to save time, Tom asked Radnor to lower a steel line which he hooked to Raymond's chains. The scientist was hauled aboard, raging at his captors.

Quickly Tom ascended the ladder. With Radnor at the controls again, the Flying Lab headed for the Citadel at top speed. Tom and Bud joined the Turnbulls in the *Sky Queen*'s lounge.

"Raymond," Tom demanded, "how did you sabotage the plant?"

"Oh, it's ingenious!" he cackled. "Oh my, yes, ingenious. Only I could have figured such a way to destroy your precious Citadel!"

Tom's patience was at an end. "What way?" he cried. "By damaging the bank of moderating rods?"

"Too crude, too crude," Raymond gloated. "I have slugged you, Tom Swift. That's what I have done. I have really slugged—"

Suddenly Raymond gasped and crumpled unconscious to the floor. Bud and Tom removed the manacles and lifted him onto a bunk.

"He'll be out for hours," Robert said. "He's had these spells on and off ever since his mind snapped."

"Then he'll never be able to tell us in time to save the plant!" Bud cried.

"He may have told us something already," mused Tom.

"What do you mean?" Robert asked.

"I'm not sure yet, and we can't take any chances. I'm going to radio ahead to Dad and have the plant evacuated."

Back at the Citadel, preparations for a mass evacuation began the moment Tom's message was received. Mr. Swift supervised the orderly withdrawal.

Wailing sirens sounded throughout the reserve, and soon buildings and dormitories were emptied of personnel. Trucks and trailers, lined up at the gate, quickly filled with workers, and security police in jeeps raced to outlying testing grounds to pick up stragglers.

Within forty-five minutes the plant was cleared. Mr. Swift, who was driving the last truck, gave the signal to move out. The convoy rolled slowly through the exit, then picked up speed. Soon the caravan, racing along at a fast clip, stretched out for five miles over the wasteland.

Moments after the evacuation, Radnor landed the *Sky Queen* vertically only a few hundred yards from the main building. The jet lifters blasted the sand beneath them into a fused glassy substance. He taxied directly to the concrete housing of the pile and Bud and Tom dropped from the plane. Dashing toward the entrance, they both stopped short. Red warning lights were on.

"The pile is in operation!" Tom exclaimed. "Raymond must have used one of his timing devices to start it. We'll never get near that oven now. If the plant is going to be saved, Ator will have to do it!"

They ran to the control house. Mr. Swift had taken the precaution of leaving the robot's control panel on stand-by, so no warm-up period was needed. Tom marched Ator to the ramp and the robot descended into the tunnel.

Transmitted through Ator's "eyes" the picture on

the television screen in the control building showed the dim underground passage, and as Tom watched the screen, the outer opening to the atomic pile appeared. With a feeling of finality Tom activated controls to close the tunnel entrance behind Ator. The robot strode past the thick foundations in the basement directly beneath the oven, then climbed the ramp leading to the atomic pile. He made his way past the breeder reactor and stood before the pile, facing the honeycomb wall.

Then, with Tom calling directions, Bud fed detailed instruction tapes into the panel. As they worked the automaton into position, Tom explained his hunch to Bud.

"When Raymond mentioned 'slugging' to me, it gave me an idea. The pile feeds on slugs of Uranium-238, which is nonfissionable. In the pile a portion of it is slowly converted into plutonium. Now if you feed the pile a slug containing a high concentration of plutonium, it could set off an explosion before the moderator material ever had a chance to quench the reaction. I think one of those slugs has been loaded with plutonium."

"But how will you know which one?" Bud queried. "They all look alike on the screen."

"The fake slug's weight will be different," Tom replied. "Ator's finger joints are highly sensitive to pressure. By comparing the weight of the slugs one against another, he'll isolate the bomb."

"That may take hours!"

"It's the only chance, Bud," Tom said quietly. "Feed in two pressure-comparison tapes."

Bud slipped the punched ribbons from their containers and reeled them on the metal pin "readers." Tom directed the basic actions and Ator began the tedious process of extricating the slugs from the oven and comparing one with another.

Hours passed as the process was repeated over and over. Precious minutes were lost when a tape broke. Tom's eyes began to sting from the strain of staring at the screen, and his fingers grew numb at the controls.

"Less than an hour to go!" Bud groaned.

Tom nodded grimly, then suddenly yelled:

"He's got it! It's one of the two he's handling now. They don't balance, so all I have to do is compare them both against one we've already tested."

"The one with the odd weight will be the phony, right?"

"Yes, and there it is!" Tom exclaimed.

The isolating process completed, an equally precarious operation remained—to dismember and disperse the miniature atom bomb. No tapes were used for this task. It was handled entirely by Tom. He worked slowly, manipulating the controls with extreme caution. More than half an hour was spent while Ator, handling flasks and reagents like a veteran chemist, carefully dissolved the lethal mass. Finally he diluted it to a safe concentration with an inert salt.

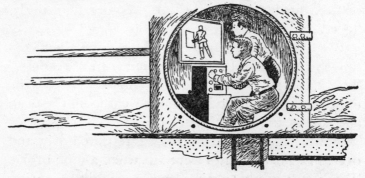

"He's got it!" Tom suddenly yelled

The Citadel had been saved!

"You did it, boy, you did it!" Bud yelled, clapping his friend on the back.

Tom grinned in relief, then said, "But I've still got work to do, Bud. Ator will have to insert inhibitor rods into the pile. Until that's done and the pile is considerably slowed down, someone will have to stay on guard."

Tom remained at the control panel while Bud went with Radnor in the *Sky Queen* to find Mr. Swift and the caravan. Within three hours the Citadel was restored to full activity.

During the two days preceding the start of formal operations, Robert Turnbull briefed the Swifts on his brother's activities since his escape from Blackstone. He confirmed Tom's theory that Raymond had used the stolen relotrol to distort Tom's control of Stan Lee, and that he had taken over the giant Ator. In his haste to move the crows' mobile control

unit, Raymond had been forced to leave the timing gear of the bank-vault door in the shack near Swift Enterprises.

With Robert's clues, police rounded up all the hirelings that had worked under the Briggin gang, including the fake magician who had wanted to rent Herbert. One of the henchmen confessed that he had dropped the small bomb on the Citadel from a high-flying jet. Another admitted that he was the stowaway who had overpowered Jones and his crew on their flight west with the cybernetic arms.

Raymond was recommitted to the institution, but specialists at Blackstone were optimistic about his complete recovery.

The day of the Citadel's opening ceremonies arrived. Tom had arranged for Phyl, Sandy, Chow, and his mother to fly out with a planeload of officials from Swift Enterprises. High government dignitaries and representatives of the Army and Navy were present as observers.

When the audience was seated before a large television screen, Tom and his father entered the control house. Mr. Swift set the cybernetic arms in operation, turning over their controls to a technician, while his son fed signal tapes to Ator's panel. Through the camera eyes of Tom's great invention, the viewers saw the nuclear quenching rods slide into place, smoothly regulating the rate of chain-reaction conversion.

"It's a complete success!" Bud cried enthusiastically as Tom and his father emerged from the building and joined the onlookers.

"Oh, Tom, I'm so proud of you," Phyl said, her eyes shining.

Mrs. Swift glowed with happiness as she looked at her husband and son.

In impressive speeches, the government officials lauded the Swifts and pointed out the tremendous advances in medicine, industry, and national defense which the products of the pile would make possible.

"Can't we see Ator?" Sandy asked.

Tom explained sadly that the now-radioactive robot must never leave the concrete-shielded pile. He would remain forever in the plant which he had helped to save.

"I reckon he's happy there," Chow reasoned. "It's home to him." The cook grinned broadly. "An' he can do his own cookin' on the 'oven'!"

"What's your next brain child going to be, Tom?" Bud asked with a grin.

Tom smiled and shrugged his shoulders, unaware at the moment that it would be his *Atomic Earth Blaster* and would lead him into one of the strangest adventures of his life.

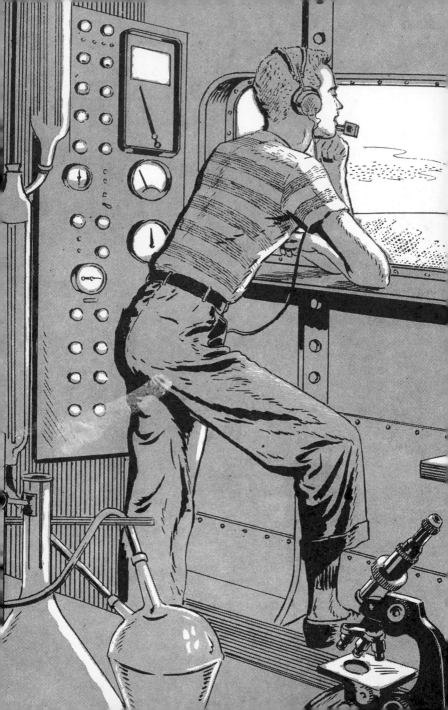